THE CANONGATE STRANGLER

THE CANONGATE STRANGLER is a psychological thriller with supernatural overtones set in Edinburgh: the wynds and closes of the Old town, the Georgian facades of the New; the pubs; the Castle; Arthur's Seat ... Edward Middleton, a respectable solicitor, finds himself strangely involved in a series of murders. Horrified, he tries first to explain, then to prevent, their headlong progress – but who is the man the press are calling 'The Canongate Strangler'?

McAllister's novel recalls Hogg and Stevenson in its preoccupations with the ambivalence of personality and identity.

Angus McAllister is a lecturer in Law at Paisley College of Technology. He is best known for his Science fiction – A VARIETY OF SENSATIONS and the SF comedy THE KRUGG SYNDROME. He has also written many short stories, including the prizewinning WHAT DREAMS MAY COME, recently published in the Scottish SF anthology Starfield. *Much of his work has been translated into German and broadcast on German radio.*

THE CANONGATE STRANGLER

by

ANGUS McALLISTER

DOG AND BONE
GLASGOW 1990

THIS NOVEL WAS
FIRST PUBLISHED
IN SCOTLAND 1990
BY
DOG & BONE
PRESS
175 QUEEN VICTORIA
DRIVE, GLASGOW
DESIGNED BY
ALASDAIR GRAY
TYPESET BY
DONALD SAUNDERS
PRINTED, BOUND
BY
COX & WYMAN,
CARDIFF RD, READING

ISBN 1 872536 10 7

THE PUBLISHERS ACKNOWLEDGE SUPPORT
FROM THE SCOTTISH ARTS COUNCIL
TOWARDS PUBLICATION OF THIS VOLUME

There was something strange in my sensations, something indescribably new, and, from its very novelty, incredibly sweet. I felt younger, lighter, happier in body; within I was conscious of a heady recklessness, a current of disordered sensual images running like a mill-race in my fancy, a solution of the bonds of obligation, an unknown but not an innocent freedom of the soul. I knew myself, at the first breath of this new life, to be more wicked, tenfold more wicked, sold a slave to my original evil; and the thought, in that moment, braced and delighted me like wine.

Robert Louis Stevenson,
Dr. Jekyll and Mr. Hyde.

TABLE OF CONTENTS

EDITOR'S PREFACE

MOST readers will be familiar with the case of the Canongate Strangler, the mass murderer who terrorised the city of Edinburgh last year. It is less well known that Henry Cunningham, the man accused of the crimes, spent much of his time while awaiting trial writing his own account of the murders. The resulting manuscript forms the bulk of this book.

It might help in assessing this rather peculiar document to have some insight into the killer's known mental condition. Cunningham had a lengthy criminal record and had been the subject of several psychiatric reports in the past. They were all agreed on the diagnosis: that he was a psychopath, or sociopathic personality.

However, although Cunningham had past convictions for crimes of violence, he had never before been accused of murder. The popular understanding of the term psychopath as a crude killer is not quite accurate. What it really means is an individual with inhibited moral development. He may be superficially charming and likeable, but he has no capacity to love or care for anyone except himself. He lacks a conscience and is free of guilt feelings. He may not kill, but should he acquire that urge, he would indulge it as readily as he would squash an insect.

This sums up Cunningham's past psychiatric history. It shows a mental condition that, while not normal, is at least fairly straightforward. The psychiatrist who attended Cunningham in prison was confronted by a more complex and inconsistent

11

personality. Sometimes the prisoner would show a callous defiance, typical of the psychopath, but at other times he professed to repent of his crimes. He also appeared to suffer from delusions and hallucinations, reality disorders not normally associated with psychopathy as such. Prominent among these was his persistent assertion that he was not Henry Cunningham at all and that the police had arrested the wrong man.

In assessing what follows, the reader should keep in mind that the psychopath is typically a compulsive liar. So it is possible that Cunningham's protestations of sanity may well be a front for a very complex subterfuge intended to prove exactly the opposite. He would certainly not be the first murderer to have faked madness.

The reader must make up his own mind. One way or another, he should find it an intriguing tale.

CUNNINGHAM'S NARRATIVE

ONE

MY NAME IS EDWARD JAMES MIDDLETON, and I am writing this narrative as a last, desperate means of establishing my true identity. For I am presently confined in a prison cell, having been mistaken for a man called Henry Cunningham, a habitual criminal and mass murderer.

I still find it impossible to accept that such an error could have occurred. Nor is it my main concern that I may have to stand trial for a series of unspeakable crimes of which I am innocent. The real horror of my situation comes from seeing the murderer walking free, taking over my life, living with my wife and family; from the hourly anticipation that those I love most may become the latest victims of his foul urges.

I realise that the above claim is a very difficult one to justify, but it is my intention in these pages to try and do so. Nevertheless, the fantastic nature of what I have to tell makes it difficult to convince even myself that my present nightmare is not a delusion, and that what I am now writing is not the ravings of a madman.

Yet *I am not mad*. That is the one conviction to which I must cling if I am to save my family. My sanity is the essential fact I must convey to the readers of this narrative. I can think of only one way to achieve this goal: I must tell my story in as reasoned and coherent a fashion as its character will allow.

As I said above, my name is Edward James Middleton. I am twenty-nine years old, have been happily married for the last five years and have two young children. I am by profession a solicitor and for several years have been a partner in Summers & Wintergreen, an established law firm in Edinburgh.

I have lived all of my life in Edinburgh, where I was brought up in a respectable middle-class family and attended one of the city's best schools. After reaching adulthood, I learned from my parents that I had been adopted at birth; however, since they could not have given more love or attention to their own child, this fact of my origin has never caused me any concern. Until the beginning of this year, my life could have been described as successful, though hardly the material of high drama.

Does this sound like the background of the notorious Canongate Strangler? Could this describe the origin of the sub-human beast that has terrorised this city for almost a year?

I must exercise more control. Even as I wrote the above, my experience as a lawyer told me that it proved nothing. It is true that poverty may substantially contribute to the incidence of crime and to the development of vicious tendencies, but a privileged background offers no immunity against such an outcome; in the many cases with which my profession has acquainted me, I have more than once seen society's weeds spring from the best-tended soil.

I am straying from the point. It is not my character that is at issue, but my identity. The good character of Edward Middleton is a matter of record; as for Henry Cunningham, the man they think they have arrested, he has earned his place in Hell as far as I am concerned, and it is no part of my purpose to try and defend him.

It was in January of this year that I experienced the first of the strange occurrences which led to my present situation. Even now, when so much has happened that is even worse, I recall that night with a feeling of unreality. It was a Sunday, and as I was to attend an important criminal hearing at the High Court next morning, I had gone to bed at around ten thirty; when there are young children in the house, one's rest is often subject to interruption, and both my wife and I had got into the habit of compensating for this by retiring early.

I soon fell asleep and am not sure how long I had been unconscious before it seemed to me that I was walking along the pavement of a main street. I recognised it as Lothian Road, less than half a mile from my home at the edge of Edinburgh New Town. To my left, the floodlit outline of Edinburgh Castle appeared in sharp relief against the black of the castle rock. The night was clear, with a slight frost, and the scarcity of people suggested it was at least the early hours of the morning. I suppose, in conventional language, this experience could only be described as a dream, though I had never known one so vivid, so logically constructed or, as I later discovered, so horribly persistent in the memory. And yet I was at the same time aware of still being at home in bed. It was as if my spirit had taken flight and was now occupying the body of another man, so that I experienced the world through his senses. I also shared his emotions, which at that moment were a mixture of tension and elation, as though some great event, both dreadful and beautiful, were about to occur.

I met a few other men on my way, but we passed as strangers, without acknowledgement. I had not yet found what I was seeking. At length I reached the Usher Hall and turned off down a side street, beside the Lyceum Theatre. At first there was not another person in sight. And then I saw at last what I had been waiting for.

I turned casually into a nearby alley, as if I were an innocent night traveller arriving home. Then I stopped and waited. The woman must have suspected nothing, for her footsteps continued to approach without hesitation. As she approached the alley, I stepped out and barred her way. "Have you got a light, dear?" I asked her.

She was a pretty girl, aged perhaps nineteen or twenty, and was smartly dressed, as if returning from an evening out. She appeared startled, which was natural enough. "I'm sorry," she said, "I don't smoke."

"I don't believe you," I said. "You've got matches in your handbag. Let me see it."

She clutched her handbag closely to her, wrongly assuming that it was the main object of my interest. It would have been better for her if it had been. Then she tried to push past me, but I easily stopped her. She began to plead with me, beginning to babble as she grew more frightened. I clasped my hand over her mouth to keep her quiet and dragged her into the alley. She did her best to resist, but I was much stronger than her. When we were well back from the street, between the stone walls of the surrounding building, I took my hand from her mouth; but, before she had the chance to utter a further sound, I had grasped her by the throat and was squeezing her life away. She continued to resist, first of all trying to push me off, but my arms were longer than hers and her blows were ineffectual; then she tried to pull my hands from her neck, but her inferior strength was already growing weaker. In the confines of the alley, surrounded by the silence of the night, her struggles seemed to make a considerable noise, but no-one came.

She did succeed in kicking me a number of times about the shins, which was quite painful. I could easily have stopped her by banging her head against the wall, but that would have finished things too quickly. Soon her resistance grew less and then stopped. I noticed that her tongue was protruding from her mouth, and fancied that her complexion had grown darker in colour, though it was difficult to tell in the light available. I continued to apply pressure, just to be sure. Finally, I let the body go and it sprawled untidily on the ground, now looking more like a piece of discarded rubbish than a human being.

I checked for a pulse, but she appeared to be dead. Her eyes were wide open, and stared at me, as if she could not quite believe what had happened. This did not bother me at all. I opened her handbag, found her purse and pocketed several banknotes and some change; robbery was not my motive, but a little extra money always comes in useful. Almost as an afterthought, I wiped both sides of the handbag with my sleeve before throwing it back beside the body; it was the only thing upon which I might have left fingerprints.

I left the alley and walked on down the street, in the

direction from which the woman had come. There was no-one in sight. My legs ached considerably from her kicking, but I did not care and the pain soon eased. I turned left at the end of the road, doubling back towards the back of the castle. By the time I met another late traveller, I was well away from the scene of the murder.

As the murderer walked quickly down the empty street, flanked by the high cliff at the rear of the castle, he began to descend from the peak of excitement that had accompanied his crime, and which had dominated my emotions while it was taking place. Now my own natural feelings began to fight for dominance over those of the man whose body I had for a time seemed to share. My revulsion at the killing took over and the dreadful vision faded. I was left sitting up in bed, beside my sleeping wife.

I had no sense of having woken from a dream; rather I seemed to have been instantly transferred, still conscious, from one location to another. I thought of the crime I had just witnessed, in which I had seemed to participate, and it took all the self-control at my command not to cry out. I saw from my bedside clock that it was just after one a.m. Leaving my wife still asleep, I slipped quietly from bed, donned my dressing gown and slippers and left the bedroom.

I checked on the children, then went to the kitchen and made myself a cup of tea. All around me, the ordinariness of my domestic setting contrasted incongruously with the scene I had just left behind. I tried to soak in the homely atmosphere, to convince myself that it had just been a nightmare; but the memory of that alley and its secret, of the dead woman's stare, followed me round the house like an accusing phantom.

Unable to banish the memory, I tried instead to make sense of it. My reason told me that it had to be a dream, but my instinct, my innermost convictions, told a different story. This was something new, something I had not experienced before.

But if it was not a dream, what had really occurred? Was I going insane? The middle of the night, when one is alone, is not the best time to entertain such thoughts. I was tempted to wake my wife Jean and share the burden, tell her what had happened and seek from her some words of reassurance. But her sleep is often enough interrupted by the more legitimate demands of the children; they might wake in the night from bad dreams and seek comfort, but that was not what she expected from her husband. I decided to postpone further speculation until the morning.

When I think of what Jean has since suffered on my account, how trivial seems the interruption of one night's rest! If I had taken that small step of waking her and confiding in her, would subsequent events have continued along the same disastrous path? I do not know, but at least I would have had an ally in the succeeding months, and might perhaps have broken free of the web that increasingly ensnared me. I did not realise it then, but that one little act of kindness, that trivial piece of considerate behaviour, caused the first crack in our relationship, which before long had widened to an unbridgeable gulf.

Finally I calmed down enough to return to bed. I eased myself in beside Jean and she slept on undisturbed. I closed my eyes and tried to sleep, but the image of the alley returned with renewed clarity. It was almost morning before exhaustion eased me into a light slumber.

TWO

I AM NOT AN EVIL MAN, nor even a particularly bad one. Like the majority of the human race, I have experienced antisocial urges, but like most respectable members of society I have learned to control them. It is true that, as a boy and in early adolescence, I showed a certain wildness of disposition, and often got into scrapes that made me the despair of my parents. However, the influence of their upbringing – strict, yet never lacking in love, caring, but never over-indulgent – saw me safely into maturity.

It may seem odd that someone with a taste for the more adventurous aspects of life should have chosen a career so apparently mundane as the law. But I wanted to please my father, himself a banker by profession, and my decision was intended partly to make amends for the trouble I had caused him in my youth. It is one of my lasting comforts that he saw me graduate from Edinburgh University before his death. Even so, after qualifying, I found myself drawn towards the drama of the courtroom rather than the more office-bound areas of legal business. And although the reality of court practice is a little less glamorous than its public image, I never regretted my decision. I was happy at my work as well as successful. The shortcomings of my youth had been truly outgrown and not merely suppressed. That is a vital point, one I must establish at the outset.

I am aware that the above may not seem entirely relevant, possibly even a little defensive. Perhaps I have just got my material out of order. Let me steer my narrative back on course. In time, the reader will understand my drift.

Things always seem better in the morning. At breakfast, reassured by the daylight, the presence of my family and the trivial chatter of the disc jockey on the local radio station, I began to believe that my experience was indeed no more than a peculiarly vivid nightmare. As the children were fed and made the usual noise in the process, the normality of the scene prevailed upon me. My morale began to improve. Nevertheless, my lack of sleep had left me with a headache and the memory of my dream was still clear enough to impair my appetite. Eventually my wife Jean remarked upon this and upon my unusual taciturnity.

"What's wrong?" she asked me. "Are you worried about the case?"

"No," I said. "It's in the High Court, so counsel will be appearing. I'll just be acting as his office boy."

"But with your usual modesty, you think you could do better than him?"

I could see that she was trying to introduce a touch of lightness into the conversation, attempting to sound out my mood. I tried to respond as normally as possible. "We're using Robertson," I said. "In his case, I don't mind admitting to being second best." I tried to think of something further to say, but failed. There was a pause.

"Ted, there *is* something wrong. What is it?"

This was my opportunity to unburden my secret. No longer would I be interrupting her sleep by doing so, and moreover she was eager to hear what I had to say. I was on the point of telling her everything, but then I looked at the children who were still happily messing about with their breakfast. Could I recount such a gruesome story within their earshot?

I decided to spare them. At the time I thought this was my real reason, but now I am less sure.

"I woke up in the middle of the night and couldn't get back to sleep," I told her. "I feel exhausted."

"That's not like you," she said. "You usually sleep well

enough. Are you feeling all right?"

"Yes. At least there's nothing a good night's rest won't cure."

"What caused you to wake up?"

"I had a nightmare."

"What was it about?"

"Nothing much. I mean, I've forgotten."

That was not true, but it stopped her interrogation for the time being. Then the eight o'clock news came on the radio, giving us both an excuse to interrupt the conversation, which was becoming a little strained. We listened together in silence to several items of national interest.

Then the newsreader said, "In Edinburgh, the body of a young woman was found this morning in an alley near the Lyceum Theatre. Police are treating the case as one of murder. The victim's name has still to be released."

After that, he went on with further items, but I did not hear them. No sooner had he begun to announce the murder, than the rest of his statement had seemed inevitable, somehow preordained. I had felt, as he spoke, that I could predict each further word, as my desperate pretence that I had merely dreamed about the murder was mercilessly stripped away. I must have said something, without being aware of it; in any event, Jean responded to my reaction in some alarm.

"Ted, what's the matter? For God's sake answer me!"

"It really happened!"

"What really happened? Did something in the news upset you? Was it the murder, was she someone you knew? How could she have been? They didn't even give her name. Ted, speak to me!"

I made an effort to bring myself under control. "It's nothing," I said. "I'm sorry."

"How can you say that? You're face is absolutely white, you're shaking all over. You're scared to death about something. What is it?"

"Something in the news reminded me of my nightmare."

"What was it? Was it the murder? Ted, where are you going?"

I had pushed back my chair and was leaving the breakfast table. "I've got to call in at the office before going to court. It's time I left."

"But it's only eight o'clock. Your office doesn't open until nine."

She followed me to the hall, still protesting, as I grabbed my jacket and coat and left the house, with scarcely a further word of explanation.

I should have said more to her, given a better explanation for my peculiar conduct. But at the time I was gripped by a single obsession: to revisit the scene of the crime, to somehow prove that what I had heard on the radio was not true.

My office is in the Old Town, within easy walking distance of my home, and it was normal for me to leave my car behind. It didn't involve much of a detour to go via Lothian Road and soon I found myself retracing the steps of my dream journey. It was a fresh bright morning, and there could not have been a greater contrast between this busy main street and the deserted road of the previous night. Yet this only seemed to highlight the ominous familiarity of the route and the certainty of what I would find at its end. The newsreader had named the very location at which I had witnessed the murder. My only hope was that I would find the police cordon round another part of the street, proving the whole business to have been a ghastly coincidence. But when I arrived, the expected crowd was gathered round the very alley in which I had committed my vicarious crime.

I approached as close as the crowd and the police barrier would allow. There was much police activity, but I could make out no detail of what was happening. I turned to my nearest neighbour. "Do you know what's going on here?" I asked him.

"A girl's been murdered," he told me, giving the information with a relish that I found distasteful. "They found her in that alley."

"Have you heard any details?"

"Not much. They say she was strangled."

He said more, but I had already begun to walk away. He

called something after me that I did not catch.

I eased my way free of the crowd, trying not to listen to the morbid and callous discussions that were going on around me. Were these people typical of the general public, or only of those who congregate at the scenes of murders? I hoped that the latter was the case. Being a criminal lawyer can give one a distorted view of human nature.

I took the shortest route to my office and, by an unnerving coincidence, found I was following the same path the murderer had taken as he left the scene of the crime. As I followed the winding road behind the castle rock, I went over and over again in my mind what had happened, trying to make sense of it, considering all possible rational (or least irrational) explanations. The easiest and most comforting – that it had been a dream – I was now forced to rule out. What possibilities were left?

Could I be psychic? I had never seen any evidence of it before and, in any case, I was not at all sure I believed in the existence of such powers. Maybe I would now have to reconsider my opinion. Or perhaps I was telepathic. Had I been reading the mind of the murderer as he committed the crime? I had never believed in telepathy either. Was it any different from being psychic? I didn't know.

There was another possible explanation, which I now realised had been growing in my subconscious for some time. It was a theory which I had been refusing to face.

Was I the murderer?

I had been convinced at the time that I was still at home in bed while the crime was being committed. Or at least that was the impression I got when I first seemed to enter the murderer's mind: afterwards, I was too engrossed with what was happening to notice. Could I have left the house and suffered a memory blackout of the periods before and after the murder? All I knew for sure was that I fell asleep shortly after ten-thirty and was back in bed by one a.m. The murder site was less than fifteen minutes walk from my home. Jean was a sound sleeper – the children had often wakened me and left her undisturbed – and she had not known of my nocturnal visit to the kitchen. I could just as easily have left the house and returned undetected.

Then another point occurred to me. The murderer had left by the route I was now taking, which was in the opposite direction to my home. But I only remembered a small part of that journey and could have doubled back later. Who knows where I might have wandered during a period of blackout?

More importantly, the killer had been repeatedly kicked by his victim. Did I have any injuries? Ignoring the curious looks of passers-by, I went quickly to the back of the pavement, lifted each of my trouser legs in turn and thoroughly examined my shins. There was no sign of bruising or any other kind of mark. I carefully felt each of my legs, but experienced no pain.

I continued my journey feeling considerably reassured, but my relief was short-lived. I did not know how badly the murderer had been injured, if at all. He had been able to ignore the pain and it had faded quickly afterwards. But would the victim's fingernails not have left scratches on his hands or forearms? I had no memory of this one way or the other. The truth of the matter was this: my lack of injury was perhaps significant, but it proved nothing.

Needless to say, I was not particularly happy with this line of reasoning. My skills in legal debate were being too well utilised towards a morbid end. I was not insane. I could not be the murderer.

But the idea remained in my mind and would not go away. It was a ridiculous explanation, but so were all the others I could think of.

Should I go to the police with my story?

Unless I was going to confess to the crime, which I would certainly not do without further evidence, what could I tell them that they would believe? Was there any useful information I could give them? I couldn't think of any.

I was now nearing my office. I had a full day's work in front of me and, in view of my lack of sleep, it would require all my concentration. It was an easy matter to postpone any further decisions for the time being.

THREE

VALERIE WAS WAITING for me when I arrived at the office. She had already sorted out my morning mail and was ready to go through it with me.

Oh Valerie, as I write this I can see you again as you were that morning! Young, beautiful, cheerful, always eager to help, the best secretary I could have wished for. And while it is my purpose in this narrative to establish my innocence, as far as you are concerned, Valerie, I admit my guilt. I still cannot bear to think of what you have suffered on my account. I never did anything knowingly to hurt you, but that does not ease my conscience.

It occurs to me that the above might be open to misinterpretation. Let me put the record straight. When I said that I was a happily married man, I told the truth. Since our marriage, I have always been faithful to my wife. I have never been with another woman, let alone been guilty of anything so crass as having an affair with my secretary. I love my wife and family and they mean more to me than anything else in the world.

If I am to be completely honest, I have to admit that I was not always so monogamous. I have always found that women were attracted to me, and in my younger days there were many occasions when I took advantage of this. But my wild oats were all sown before my marriage, and I have never looked back since.

That does not mean that illicit thoughts have never entered

my mind. I will even admit that I had entertained such notions about Valerie. What man would not, with such a lovely girl? I also fancied that I would not have found her unwilling, had I done anything about it. But I never did.

The reader may think I am protesting too much. Well, so be it. It is no part of my purpose to prove myself to be a saint. I have no objection to being seen as a weak human being like any other. My only aim is to clear myself of the monstrous crimes of which I have been accused.

By the time I arrived at the office it was ten minutes past nine and Valerie was waiting with my mail. It was not long before I was due in court, but so much of my time is spent there that I have to make maximum use of any odd hours I can snatch to keep my desk clear.

"Anything important?" I asked her.

"Mostly routine. There's a letter about the Morris case, from the insurance company's lawyers. They think it's a case of arson."

"They would. I'll deal with that later. Anything else?"

"A few legal aid applications have come through. I think I can handle them. Oh, and your tickets for the Faculty Dinner have arrived."

"Good. Jean's been asking about them. I can't think why, she was bored to death last year."

Valerie smiled. It was a lovely smile. It had often seemed to me that I could do no wrong in her eyes. I dictated a few routine letters, gave her instructions about how to deal with the others, then gathered together my papers for the High Court case. Valerie had them all ready for me. One of her main functions was to keep me free of tedious administrative work, for which I have little time and even less inclination. By ten to ten I was ready to leave for the court.

It was a murder case that I was attending. This was a coincidence that had already troubled me.

"How do you think it'll go?" Valerie asked me.

"He's admitted doing it, so he won't get off. But I reckon Robertson will get it reduced to culpable homicide."

"Will it be finished today?"

"I should think so, but keep me clear of appointments tomorrow just in case."

"Poor man, I feel sorry for him. You can see how he must have been provoked. Now that murder last night, that was a different matter. Did you hear about it? What's the matter Mr. Middleton, did I say something to startle you?"

"No, it's all right."

"Wasn't it terrible? They found a girl strangled this morning, just off Lothian Road. She was lying in an alley, just across from— "

"I know, I was— I mean, I heard something about it on the news."

"I hope they catch him soon. They should bring back hanging for people like that. Are you all right, Mr. Middleton? You've gone all white."

"I'm OK. I didn't sleep very well last night." I put the papers in my briefcase and began to make my way out. "I'll phone you later and let you know how it's going."

I was glad to get back out in the fresh air and felt the better of the short walk to the court. It was not only Valerie's reference to the murder that had distressed me, but all through our conversation I had been haunted by a resemblance between her and the murdered girl. I had imagined that young body, so full of life, lying crumpled and abandoned in a dark alley, those lively eyes wide and staring at me in silent accusation. In truth, I had no clear memory of what the dead girl looked like while alive, and I am sure the resemblance had been imposed after the event by my troubled mind. But I could still not get it out of my head.

Unfortunately, the case was not of a type to help me forget my preoccupation. It concerned a man who had battered his wife to death. He had not meant to kill her, there was evidence that he had been severely provoked, and in most ways the circumstances were quite different from the callous act I had witnessed the night before. All the same, I was glad that Robertson, our counsel, was the one taking the active role and that I was merely subsidiary. The worst moment was when the police doctor took the stand and went into great clinical detail about the injuries that had caused the woman's death. In my imagination I was seeing other injuries, equally lethal, being imposed on another body, in another location. I became overcome by such nausea that I had temporarily to leave the court to seek some air.

Robertson was curious about my behaviour and quizzed me about it over lunch. Robertson is a slight man in his early forties, an accomplished advocate whose off-stage performance is equally smooth. I usually found his cynical conversation amusing, but not on this occasion.

"Well what do you think Ted? Five years? Six?"

"Probably."

"A pity really. In the old days they'd have strung him up, just to keep down the prison population. Not such a bad idea, when you come to think of it."

My client could not have had a better man to defend him, but not from any goodwill on Robertson's part. If he had been prosecuting, he'd have been just as happy to get the poor man life. "That's not very fair," I said. "It wasn't entirely his fault."

"Who said it was? You're missing the point. So we do our best for him and what happens? In a few years he's back in the dole queue. Come on Ted, he's not exactly an asset to society. I don't suppose his wife was either, for that matter."

"So do you think hanging would be a deterrent?"

Robertson laughed. "Of course not. Do you think I'd recommend something that would scare off potential clients? It's just that we might as well take the chance to be shot of pathetic little buggers like him. There are plenty more where he came from."

The waiter brought the wine and Robertson volunteered to taste it. He had chosen the wine, as well as the restaurant, both being suitably expensive. My job was merely to foot the bill. By now he had finished his French onion soup, and continued to enjoy his free lunch as the waiter returned with his veal and a choice of vegetables. "Yes it's not a bad place this," he said. "What's the matter with you, Ted? You don't seem to have much of an appetite."

"I'm all right."

"You could have fooled me. What were you up to this morning, rushing out of court like that?"

"Nothing, I just needed a bit of fresh air."

"I thought the boredom must have got to you. That's the real trouble with this case, it's so damn ordinary. We could do with something a bit more lively. Now that dead girl they found this morning, that sounds a bit more like the thing. Could be a repeater, maybe even another Ripper case. Just what we need, eh Ted? We might even consider giving him a discount for bulk killing."

"For God's sake!" I put down my knife and fork and pushed my plate away. My steak – medium-rare, the way I usually like it – stared back at me like a butchered corpse. The little food I had eaten began to rise in my stomach, then settled down again. I lifted my wine glass and drained its contents in a gulp.

Robertson looked at me, half concerned, half amused. "You really aren't your usual self. If I didn't know you better, I'd think the case was getting to you."

"I'm all right. Maybe we should just change the subject."

"All right by me. Anyway, I'm glad you like the wine. I think it's one of my better choices."

"It should be, it certainly costs enough."

Robertson chuckled. "Come off it, Ted. You know you use my lunches as a tax loss."

After that the conversation settled into safer areas, and my appetite partially returned.

In the afternoon, the jury took very little time to find our client guilty of culpable homicide; then the judge jailed him for five years and the case was over by four o'clock. My client was taken off for his enforced repentance and Robertson also took his leave, a satisfied technician who had completed another routine assignment. I telephoned Valerie to tell her the news, and said that I was going straight home.

This was unlike my usual practice – there was bound to be something for me to do in the office, if only a few letters to sign – but I had no stomach for any further business that day. Instead I bought an evening paper and kept on walking until I was out of the area where I might run into legal colleagues. Then I went into the first pub I came to.

I bought myself a double gin and tonic, then quickly looked through the paper. The murder had secured about a third of a column on page three, a paltry coverage it seemed to me. For some reason I felt slightly cheated, though I am not sure why. Whatever the reason, I would not feel that way again; none of the other murders were to fare so badly in the public attention.

The article named the girl as Janet Brown, aged 21, a student who had lived in the Morningside area of the city. She had been at a disco and had been last seen alive by one of her friends only a few hundred yards from the place she was found; she had left her friend to make her way to Lothian Road, where she had hoped to pick up a taxi.

In other words, she had only risked walking alone for a very short distance. But it had been long enough to fall foul of the strangler.

There was little more to the article, beyond a few extra details about her background. There would be much more later. But it was enough to attach a name and a life to the dead face that was still lodged in my memory, and this only served to make things worse.

I ordered another double, had a quick look through the rest of the paper, then put it in my pocket. I was surrounded on all sides by lively chatter, frequent laughter, the electronic music from a gambling machine. In one corner, a silent television showed an American TV comedy being manically enacted in mime. From a jukebox, a girl was singing a sentimental love ballad. I finished my drink quickly and left for home.

I am not a regular drinker and found that the gins had gone slightly to my head. As I walked through this beautiful city, where historic buildings and monuments greet one at almost every step, my surroundings took on, in the dusk, an unreal, almost sinister aspect. I was about halfway home when it began to rain. I was wearing my coat, but had left my umbrella at home. I could easily have hailed a taxi, but I walked on. The rain got heavier, but what were a few wet clothes compared with the fate of that innocent girl?

My wife did not quite see it in the same light.

"For God's sake, Ted, you're completely soaked."

"It's nothing."

"What do you mean? You'll catch pneumonia."

"I'll go up and change." By way of a peace offering, I kissed her, then began to leave the room.

"You've been drinking!"

"Robertson did a good job. I took him out for a quick one."

"Doesn't he get paid enough?"

"We only had a couple. Anyway, we use him as a tax loss."

I went upstairs and changed out of my wet clothes. When I came back down, Jean had decided to drop her interrogation. If she had persisted at that time, I think I would have told her everything. But she is not really a nag by nature, and had decided, I think, to leave it up to me to confide in her if the need arose. Afterwards, with the children around, an opportune moment didn't really present itself. Besides, there was nothing I wanted more than to banish the matter from my mind. So I let it drop.

FOUR

I HAD STILL MADE NO DECISION about going to the police. I thought about it often, but could come to no firm conclusion. If I was not the killer, there was little I could tell them that they didn't know already, and the fact that I knew so much and had no alibi might lead them to doubt my innocence. If I *was* the killer — But I could not really believe that. Eventually I had procrastinated for so long that my delay in coming forward would have been difficult to excuse. I decided to try and forget the matter.

I didn't entirely succeed, but in the weeks that followed the affair began gradually to occupy a much less prominent part in my mind. The passage of time, involvement with my daily routine, the absence of any further strange experiences, all combined to help it fade into the background. The press carried an occasional note, mainly to the effect that the killer had not been found, but otherwise public interest began to fade. About three weeks after the murder, it abruptly revived again, along with my own involvement.

It was the night of the annual Faculty Dinner, at which the solicitors of Edinburgh took over the function suite of a top hotel. There they ate and drank well, listened to speeches from judges, Queen's Counsel and other distinguished guests, and generally pretended to enjoy themselves and appear human. I was present with my wife, and the evening proceeded predictably enough until about one a.m. By that time the company was gradually thinning, leaving only those determined to take full

32

advantage of the late bar. Jean and I were sitting with another couple, Tom and Eileen Agnew. I remember that Tom was a little drunk and that he was dominating the conversation with one of his hobby-horses.

These were my last substantial memories of the hotel suite until I recovered from my faint. From what I later heard of my behaviour, it was natural that those around me should have been surprised and alarmed. But what occurred in my mind was far more startling, and much more sinister.

I'd had a moderate amount to drink and was in a relaxed mood. The evening had been pleasant, but not over-exciting. It was not that type of evening. I was not desperate to stay much longer, but neither was I in any hurry to go home. It could be said that my emotions were in neutral gear. It was while in that condition that I began to notice the intrusion of a different feeling, one quite unrelated to my immediate environment. It was one of excitement, of anticipation, and was gradually growing in intensity. I looked around the room and the scattering of semi-drunken lawyers there, but saw nothing to account for the sensation. This did not surprise me for I had recognised the emotion and was beginning to suspect its cause.

At first I noticed nothing further. Then I became aware of a periodic interference with my vision, mainly from flashes of light. There was also a growing background noise, which I could not quite identify, but which did not belong with the sounds in the hotel. These persisted, along with the heightening tension, and before long I had formed a theory about what was happening. The hotel suite was fairly well lit, and this had been obscuring things. I waited until I thought that the attention of my table companions was fixed elsewhere, then shut my eyes.

Immediately, the vision became coherent and sprang to life. I was walking along the pavement of a back street; it was not one I recognised, but I felt sure that it was in Edinburgh, not too far away. The flashes had been from street lamps, and an occasional lighted window. The sounds had been made by my own footsteps, by the wind and, now and again, by the noise of a passing vehicle. I was a hunter on the prowl, on the lookout

33

for fresh prey.

"Are you feeling tired, Ted?"

It was Jean's voice. With some irritation, I opened my eyes. "Just a little," I said.

"Our conversation must have put him to sleep," said Tom Agnew.

"I'm not surprised," said his wife.

I smiled, but didn't deny the charge. It was a more socially acceptable explanation than the real one.

"Are you ready to go home?" asked Jean.

"There's no hurry," I said.

After that, their attention was diverted by the continuation of Tom's drunken monologue. I didn't shut my eyes again but, now that I had got my bearings, I was able to make out more of what was happening in that city street not far away. To boost the image, I tried to keep my eyes away from the most direct lighting in the room; also, as my superimposed excitement continued to increase, so the vision intensified. Finally, I left the back street and entered a broad, well-lit main road. I recognised it as Nicholson Street, on the south side of the city centre, which I was walking towards. By now I was completely caught up in the thrill of the chase, and the sights and sounds of the hotel room were merely a background interference.

Unfortunately, my companions would not let me roam the city in peace and persisted in competing for my attention. I found myself involved in a strange duality of experience, as I was continually dragged away from my adventure to indulge in polite conversation, an intrusion as irritating as it was incongruous. I find it difficult to think of a way to adequately set down what next occurred, but I will try to find an appropriate form:

I am walking down Nicholson Street, bright from superior street lighting and the illuminated displays in shop windows. It is a dry night, the first for several days, and that is what has attracted me out tonight. I like to take my pleasures in reasonable comfort. It is quiet, but there are still too many people around for my purpose. I sigh in exasperation. No-one at all in the back streets and here there are too many. A car passes me, then another, going in the opposite direction. A taxi emerges from a side street, turns and accelerates away from the city centre. I must return to somewhere more secluded. My tension increases, becomes unbearable, explodes into frustration. I walk more quickly, cross the street, pass Edinburgh University—

TOM AGNEW: Well, all I can say is, those who think being a lawyer means easy money just don't know what they're talking about. They haven't a clue.

EILEEN AGNEW: Yes I know, dear. It's terrible being on the breadline.

TOM: I'm not kidding. We might have had it good once, but not any more. There's a glut of lawyers on the market, and half of them are a bunch of toe-rags. Just look about you, for God's sake. Look at them! There's a few here we'll soon be reading about in the Sunday papers. I remember when—

EILEEN: Keep your voice down! Anyway, you've already told us all this.

TOM: Have I? Well then, it must be true. Ted agrees with me, don't you Ted?

JEAN: Ted?

TOM: He looks as if he's miles away. Hullo Ted, are you still with us?

MYSELF: What?

TOM: Never mind. What was I saying? Yes, there's no money in it any more. Take conveyancing. Used to be a dawdle, money for old rope. Now there's all that new legislation and everybody chasing after the same business. But all Joe Public does is look at the bill and moan. He thinks it all goes straight into your pocket. What does he know about overheads – rent, rates, salaries, electricity and — and bloody rates!

EILEEN: You mentioned rates twice.

TOM: They feel like that when you're paying them. And what about insurance? Professional negligence cover. All those idiots being sued because they don't know their arse from their elbow, all those buggers with their grubby little paws in the till and the rest of us have to—

I have now reached a point where the road crosses a bridge. I stop and look over the parapet. Beneath me, like a slow moving river, passes another, much darker street. A lot more promising. How do I get down? There are no steps. I will have to go further down the road I am on, then double back. My frustration, temporarily at bay, mounts once more to a peak. I proceed along the street, quickening my step, resisting the impulse to break into a run. Can't draw unnecessary attention to myself. At last I reach a corner, do a U-turn round the back of a church, and now I am walking downhill, back towards the lower street. Already it is darker and I am alone again. My impatience subsides just a little. I reach the foot of the hill. Above me is the bridge I looked down from a few moments before. To the right are warehouses and a few pubs, long since closed for the night. I turn left, under the bridge. My alter-ego, the hotel room observer, recognises the street as the Cowgate. Here we are on a lower level of the Old Town, where once the poorer classes were kept, out of sight of their betters. Here it is much darker. As if a torch is being shone in my face, the hotel suite and its irrelevant dinner party has again imposed itself upon my vision. But I am being guided by other eyes, conveyed by other legs, and I do not falter. Drawing upon my knowledge of the city, I fill in the gaps in the picture and try to ignore the distraction. I walk on down the road. Now it is too quiet again and there is no-one at all. Then I hear footsteps approach and I hide in a dark doorway. The footsteps get nearer, there are two pairs of them. A girl passes, but she is accompanied by a man. My exasperation builds up, escalates to boiling point.

TOM AGNEW: What's the matter Ted, did I say something wrong?

MYSELF: What? No, it's all right.

TOM: For a moment, you looked as if you wanted to murder me.

EILEEN AGNEW: I'm not surprised. I was beginning to feel the same way.

TOM: It's not worth it, the insurance wouldn't pay out. Anyway, as I was saying, there's no money in law any more. Do you know what I'd do if I was starting out again? Become a chartered surveyor. I'm telling you—

EILEEN: Oh God, he's off again! We've heard it all before.

TOM: — they're the biggest crowd of chancers on the face of the Earth. All brass neck and no brains—

EILEEN: That would suit you all right.

TOM: — and they're making a fortune. Or maybe I should do the same as Ted and defend the Great Unwashed at the taxpayer's expense. Keep the streets safe for murderers and muggers, help the burglars to walk away scot-free. On the other hand, maybe it's more honourable being a capitalist leech. What do you think, Ted? Ted! Wake up!

JEAN: What's the matter, Ted?

MYSELF: Nothing. I'm all right.

Now I am in a residential area. Surely here there will be pickings? But the street is deserted. A small diversion would take me up to the Canongate, but again there might be too many people. I carry on in the same direction, the houses get sparser, and I am approaching Holyrood Park, the dark shadow of Arthur's Seat looming up on my right. Still no-one in sight. I stop and almost shout aloud in my frustration. What should I do? I hesitate for a few moments, partly releasing the pressure with inward curses, then begin to retrace my steps. Soon I am back near the houses. I walk into a side street, a dark dead end, and wait for a while. Perhaps my prey will come to me. No-one comes. Around me the dinner party babbles, the hotel lights fog my vision. But my other ears are tuned to the silence of the empty street, my other eyes adjusted to the dark. Still they pick up nothing. But people live in this area. Surely some late homecomer will appear? Again my aggravation mounts. I am not a patient man, much much less so in this alter-ego.

TOM: There's no need to look so disgusted Ted. You're doing a great job, you really are.

EILEEN: He's still not with us. I can't really say I blame him.

JEAN: Is there something wrong, Ted? Ted? Answer me, Ted. Are you all right?

MYSELF: Yes, I'm fine.

JEAN: You don't sound it. Are you sure?

MYSELF: I told you I'm all right! For Christ's sake shut your mouth!

For the time being the distracting babble is silenced. I continue my vigil until the pain of the waiting becomes almost unbearable. I light a cigarette, smoke half of it, then savagely stamp it into the ground. I am still alone. I light another cigarette and smoke it more slowly. Then, in the distance, I hear footsteps. I hold my breath and listen. Only one person. Impatience turns to excitement, almost reaching a frenzy. What if it is a man? Will I go ahead? No, men are too strong, and, in any case, the thrill would be less. But the quickness of the step, the click of the heels suggests a woman. The steps grow louder, come nearer, a figure passes across the entrance of my alley. A woman and she is young. Good. I let her pass, then follow her out into the street. Her pace quickens. I look in front of me and behind me. No-one else in sight. I hurry after her. "Excuse me, dear." She speeds up, breaks into a run. "It's all right, I won't hurt you." But she carries on. I run after her, quickly catching up. I grab her by the hair, shut in her scream with my other hand, pull her down on to the pavement. I had intended dragging her into my side street, but now that is too far back. But who cares? There is no-one around. I pull her round to face me, so that I can see the fear in her eyes as she dies. Now my hands are on her throat and I am squeezing the breath from her body. Around me there are lights, some kind of commotion, my name is being called, but my other eyes and ears are blind and deaf to it. She struggles fiercely, gouging blood from my knuckles with her fingernails. She kicks me in the groin. Pain, pain, searing pain. The bitch bitch bitch. I bang her head on the pavement, savagely, again and again and again. I continue to squeeze her throat, long after all movement has ceased. Then I stop. She is dead. I look down on what I have done. In the hotel suite, so far away, I clasp my hands over my eyes, shutting out the lights, so that I can clearly see, in that dark street, the result of my handiwork. Her eyes stare, there is froth on her lips, a pool of blood widens round her head like a dark halo. She is dead. What have I done? I have taken a human life. Why, for God's sake why, why, why? Disgust and revulsion rise within me, with a force equal to my earlier homicidal lust. My emotions are forced upon the murderer, our mental link becomes a two-way one, he is now aware of me for the first time. As he hurries away, he is stopped short by the blast of my fury. I command him to look back, and I catch a last sight of that pathetic, crumpled body lying alone on the pavement. Did I do that? Oh no no no no no no no! I hear the murderer run off as blackness comes.

FIVE

I CAME TO, lying on the floor, with Jean and Tom Agnew bending anxiously over me. Several other onlookers stood by at a discreet distance. My clothing had been loosened round about my neck. "What happened?" I asked.

"You fainted," said Tom. "Gave us a hell of a fright."

"How do you feel?" asked Jean.

"I don't know." This was literally the case. My condition, both mental and physical, was completely unfamiliar. I looked around at the normality of my surroundings and gained some reassurance. At least I had achieved some sort of stasis. Then I remembered the scene I had just left. I tried to sit upright, and was restrained by Tom and Jean.

"Steady on," said Tom. "Take it easy, mate."

I did as I was told, sipped a brandy that Tom brought me and tried to relax. What else could I do? My companions helped me up and I sat down again at the table. The onlookers began to disperse.

Some desultory small talk began. Then Tom said, "What the hell got into you, man? You were carrying on as if the devil had possessed you."

"Shut up," said his wife. "You've had too much to drink."

"No," I said. "It's all right. I want to know what happened."

Between them they described my behaviour as it had appeared to them. They first of all noticed that I had gone remarkably quiet, and then that my face had lost colour and I was staring into space. When addressed I replied in monosyllables or not at all,

40

at one point being uncharacteristically rude to Jean. Then I had begun to laugh in an hysterical, demoniacal fashion, starting quietly and escalating to a climax, all the time gripping the table as if I were trying to break it with my bare hands. Eventually my laughter had stopped in mid-flight, to be followed by a moan of despair and a continuous sobbing, during which I held my hands clasped over my eyes. Finally, I had dropped in a faint.

I could see that they were looking for an explanation, but what could I tell them? "I must have had too much to drink," I said.

They still weren't satisfied, but tactfully dropped the subject. Fortunately, the few remaining guests seemed to have forgotten about it. Eileen Agnew offered to run us home, which we gladly accepted. Neither she nor her husband made any further reference to the incident, and Jean was unusually quiet throughout the journey.

I was not fooled by her silence and, sure enough, after we reached home and the baby sitter had gone, she raised the matter again. "How are you feeling now?"

"I'm fine. Really I am."

"All right, so maybe you can tell me what the hell got into you."

"I told you. I must have had too much to drink. And it was really hot in there."

"Nonsense, you didn't have too much. You're perfectly sober now. And anyway, that wouldn't be enough to explain the way you carried on."

"Did I make a fool of myself?"

"You did, rather. But don't worry, apart from Tom and Eileen I don't think anyone else noticed too much. There weren't all that many guests left and a lot of them were under the weather."

"That's all right then."

"No it isn't. Ted, what's the matter with you? You haven't been yourself lately, not since that time when you had the nightmare. Is that what happened tonight? Did you have another one?"

"Don't be silly. I wasn't asleep."

"Then what was it, for God's sake?"

"I don't know, but I'm all right now. Let's forget it."

I could understand why Jean was so concerned and I wanted to put her mind at rest. But how could I tell her the truth? That while I had been sitting with my wife and friends, relaxing and chatting after a good dinner, I had simultaneously been prowling the streets of Edinburgh Old Town, searching the narrow wynds and closes and darkened stairways for my second victim; that eventually I had found her; that while surrounded by social chit-chat, I had had my hands round a young girl's throat, squeezing the breath from her body.

Could I have told her that? Well, perhaps I might have, had there been nothing else. She deserved an explanation and there was no other adequate one I could give. If I had told her about the murder at that time, she might have thought me mad, but when my story was confirmed by the morning news she would have been forced to take me seriously.

No, there was another reason for my silence. What I could not tell her, what I could not admit to anyone, was the feelings the crime had awakened in me. How, along with the murderer, I had been caught up in the excitement of the hunt; how I had exulted in the sense of power as the victim fought under my grip; how I too felt the elation and pure, guilt-free joy as the last spark of life was snuffed out. When the same feelings had been present at the first murder, I had attributed them entirely to the killer. But this time I could not deceive myself. Perhaps because my sensibilities were dulled by alcohol, I had let my defences fall and had shared fully in his pleasure.

How could I explain this to anyone, even my wife? It was only reluctantly, and with the greatest self-loathing, that I was able to admit it to myself.

SIX

NEXT MORNING, Jean made no further reference to the incident. However, my evasiveness was causing a degree of reserve to creep into our relationship, something that had never been there before. This upset me, but the only remedy I could think of was to sit the matter out and hope things would get better.

I listened to the news on the radio without the slightest doubt about what I would hear there. I was not mistaken. This time the item was given more prominence; even the sparse details released to the press were enough to link it with the previous unsolved crime and suggest a possible trend. I tried to remain impassive during the bulletin, and not react in any way that Jean would notice; after all, it had been after the announcement of the first murder that my peculiar behaviour had started. I am not sure how successful I was, because even that brief news item brought to life, like an action replay, the hideous images of the previous night's excursion and fanned to furnace heat the flames of my self-recrimination. But if she noticed anything she did not comment on it. Certainly there is no way that she could have suspected my prior knowledge of the crime.

However, this latest abomination had at least cleared up one point. When the murder was committed, I had been in full view of a number of reliable witnesses. So, however involved I felt, I could not possibly be the murderer. And I had an unshakeable alibi that would clear me of any suspicion. It was therefore safe for me to go to the police.

Such was my horror at the killing, that I was left with no taste for procrastination with regard to my duty. Nevertheless, for reasons that are easy to guess, it was not a visit I looked forward to.

My reservations proved to be well founded.

I left home, supposedly for the office, at my usual time. However, I made instead for the city's main police head-quarters, a place I had come to know well in the course of my profession; on that particular morning I could have wished for greater anonymity, but there was nothing else for it. When I was nearly there, I stopped at a public telephone and called Valerie to tell her I would be in late.

My legal background at least made it easier for me to get a hearing. Before long I was being shown into the office of Detective Chief Superintendant Montgomery, the officer in charge of the investigation. We had not met before, though I knew of him by reputation; the killings had obviously made a big enough impact to merit being dealt with at the highest level.

Montgomery proved to be a medium-sized man in his late forties. He was plain spoken and ordinary in appearance, both of which I suspected to be deceptive. I have since been proved right. He greeted me courteously enough, but with ill-concealed curiosity, and did not waste much time on pleasantries before getting to the point.

"I believe you have information about last night's murder?"

"Yes." I hesitated.

"Well?"

I am not sure what sort of information he expected from me. He possibly knew that I had defended many criminals; perhaps he thought that I had reason to suspect a former client. But, although his expression gave very little away, I could see that what I *did* say took him completely by surprise.

"I saw it happen," I said.

For a while he made no reply, but merely looked at me. "You mean you were there?" he asked finally.

"Not exactly."

"You weren't there, but you saw it happen?"

"Yes. It's difficult to explain."

"I can see that, but I think you should try. Why are you only reporting it now?"

Why indeed? If I had reported the killing immediately, they might not at first have taken me seriously, but would have been forced to do so when the body was found. But at the time this had not occurred to me as an option; certain as I had been that the murder was real, I had still needed the confirmation of the radio report before taking action. I saw now that this delay, instead of backing up my story, had been fatal to its credibility.

"Never mind," said Montgomery, misinterpreting the reason for my hesitation. "At least you're here now. Can you describe the killer?"

"Not really."

"I thought you saw him."

"It was dark."

"You must have noticed *something*? Was it a man or a woman?"

"A man."

"Was he tall or short, fat or thin, old or young, black or white? How long was his hair? What were his clothes like? Did you hear him speak? What kind of accent did he have?"

"I can't describe him. But I did hear him speak. I think he had a Glasgow accent."

Detective Chief Superintendant Montgomery's professional courtesy was beginning to wear a little thin. "You don't know what he looked like, but he had a Glasgow accent. That narrows down the suspects to about three quarters of a million. You still haven't told me how you came to witness the murder."

By now I greatly regretted my decision to go there. I don't think I had ever before felt such embarrassment. But I had gone too far to escape now.

"As I said, it's difficult to explain. I wasn't exactly there. I didn't actually see him. It was as if I was reading his mind. More than that, I seemed to be sharing his experiences, seeing and hearing everything that he did. I know it sounds crazy and

I don't know how it's possible, but— "

The Chief Superintendant had fixed upon me a look which I could not quite interpret, but it was enough to silence me.

"Are you telling me," he said, "that you had some kind of vision?"

"That's right. I saw the first murder too."

"Oh you did? Were you there, or did you have another supernatural experience?"

"It happened in the same way."

"Why didn't you report it?"

"I didn't think you'd believe me."

Montgomery laughed, but he didn't sound amused. "Mr. Middleton, at last you've said something that I can completely agree with." He stood up. "I think this has gone on long enough."

"But I'm telling you the truth. I did see the murder last night. I could take you to the place where it happened. I can describe the girl."

"Anyone who heard the radio this morning knows where it happened. Even now there's a crowd of ghouls ringed round the spot. For all I know, you might have been one of them before you came here. And we don't need a description of the girl. We can go down to the mortuary and look at her for ourselves."

"But— "

"I only agreed to see you because you're supposed to be a respectable member of the legal profession. I now see I made a mistake. I've already had one nutter in this morning confessing to the murder. I don't need another."

"I wasn't confessing to it."

"You might as well have been. Since you're a lawyer, I shouldn't have to tell you that you could be charged for wasting police time. Goodbye, Mr. Middleton."

I remained sitting in front of his desk, for the moment unable to move, but not knowing what else I could say. Montgomery remained standing, looking down at me, his impatience growing.

"If you have a vision of a murder *before* it happens," he

46

said, "maybe then you can let me know. On the other hand, don't bother. Can you see yourself out, or do you need an escort?"

I left the building feeling completely humiliated. Then, as I neared my office, I found that another emotion was beginning to take over.

I felt profoundly relieved, as if a great burden had been lifted from my back. I had done my duty. Was it my fault if they didn't believe me? I was discharged of all responsibility.

I am not sure if this was an attitude to be proud of. But at the time it made a welcome change.

SEVEN

IN DUE COURSE the latest victim was named as Sarah Lawson, a shop assistant, aged twenty two. She had been about to be married in a few weeks time and the popular press, in a much more extended coverage than they had given the first murder, made much of this, featuring interviews with her grieving parents and fiancé. None of this helped me to banish the experience from my mind.

Nor did public interest in the killings fade this time, as it had done before. The similarity between the two crimes and the absence of any apparent motive, or connection between the victims, made it clear that an insane killer was at large, and the public and press reacted accordingly. They believed that he would strike again, and they were not disappointed. Because of the location of the second murder, within a short distance of the Royal Mile, the killer was nicknamed the Canongate Strangler, though none of his other murders were committed in that area. That would have been difficult, even for one so cunning and so careless of his personal safety as I knew the murderer to be. For any few women who might once have ventured alone at night among the dark lanes and tall 18th Century buildings of the Old Town were now thinking better of it, and the increased police presence was never far away.

Meanwhile, with as little success as the police, I was entertaining my own speculations about the killer. Who was he? Why had I been been chosen to eavesdrop upon his vile pleasures? Was I the only one to be given this unwanted privilege? Was his the only mind I could read? And why had these extra-sensory powers of mine never been in evidence before? I had noted, from the few words I heard the killer speak, that he had a Glasgow accent; perhaps there was a geographical limit to our mental link and he had only recently moved into the Edinburgh area.

I had many questions, but very few answers. I began to realise how little help I could have been to the police, even if they had believed me, and this eased my conscience a little.

However, I did come to one resolution about which I was firm: if he tried to kill again – and, like everyone else, I was sure he would – I would do everything in my power to prevent the murder.

Otherwise, my life returned almost to normal. The tension at home began to ease, and I spent my days defending unfortunates whose crimes seemed insignificant compared to those of the fiend with whom I had been partnered. Then, a few weeks after the second murder, in the early hours of a Saturday morning, came the event I had feared; and, as before, the killer was considerate enough to take me along with him. He was also good enough to relieve me of my moral responsibility.

I seemed to be in a bar, somewhere in Edinburgh. The style was of late Victorian opulence – high ceilings with intricate cornicing, stained glass windows, wall panelling of carved wood – although I cannot remember any features that would have precisely identified the place. It was in fine condition, with no indication of a century's slide from imperial greatness. The smell of money permeated the atmosphere, in the fittings of the room, the clothes of the occupants, the accents around me. This was the haunt of stockbrokers, lawyers, accountants, merchant bankers; in other words, I was among my own kind, and I felt completely at home.

The elegantly dressed young woman beside me matched the surroundings perfectly. She was beautiful and I felt relaxed in her presence, happy to be in her company. She sat close beside me and we held hands; this gave me a feeling of both comfort and excitement. I knew who she was, of course; I had known all along, and there was no moment when it could be said to have actually come to my notice.

"This is a nice place," Valerie said. "Thank you for bringing me here, Ted."

"I wanted to. I've wanted to for a while."

"Why didn't you ask me before?"

"I don't know." I spoke the truth. Why had I never asked her out before? Why had I held back from something so natural, so inevitable? It seemed that there had been a barrier between us, but now I couldn't think what it was.

"Well you're here now," she said, and snuggled even more close to me.

We sipped our expensive drinks and enjoyed each other's presence in silence for a while. Around us, the middle-class voices pursued their middle-class themes.

"Do you suppose the children will be all right?"

"The children?"

I turned to face her again and saw that the woman beside me was Jean, my wife. Her identity didn't exactly come as a surprise, but I felt that there was something missing, something that I had lost. The sense of intimacy had waned a little; it was still there, but felt more mundane, holding less promise.

"I expect they're fine," I said.

"Is something wrong, Ted?"

"No. That is, I don't think so. Wasn't there someone else with us a moment ago?"

"There's only you and me. Something is the matter. What is it?"

This seemed like a question she had been asking me continuously for a very long time, a repetitive, nagging interrogation. "I told you it's nothing," I said roughly. "I'm going for a piss."

As I left the table, she smiled at me sweetly, as though my answer had settled all her doubts.

I made my way between the tables, looking for the toilet, but I couldn't find it. The room seemed bigger than before, and to be extending itself as I proceeded on my way. I found several promising doors, but each said Private or Manager's Office. I asked a number of people for directions, but they all looked at me coldly, as if I were something unclean; apparently nothing as vulgar as urination went on in these premises. Without being aware that I had come in a circle, I found myself passing Jean's table again; Valerie was now sitting beside her and they both waved to me as I went past. I waved back to them and wanted to rejoin them, but there was a crowd of people between us and they were out of reach. In any case, I now had a more important purpose, a more urgent need.

I carried on my way, still meeting with no success. The room now seemed to have taken on vast proportions, the babble around me became more insistent, working-class accents mixed with those of their betters. Then I found myself in an area where the room narrowed into a dark bottleneck. I arrived at a dim corner, where the ceiling was lower, the walls closer together.

"Do you know where the Gents is, pal?" I asked a little man in a dirty anorak.

"Aye, it's over there, son," he said. "Just past the fruit machine."

I went in the direction indicated. The gambling machine, with its coloured, flashing lights, was a landmark in the gloom; a middle-aged woman, shabbily dressed, was playing it obsessively. I opened a door with a frosted-glass panel and entered a small toilet with walls of dirty plaster and cracked tile. There were two tiny wash basins, one with a bowl that had been smashed, leaving only a rim with a jagged border, like the shell of a hatched egg. The door of the WC lay open, showing a bowl with no seat and a portion of wall where the bare brick was exposed. The air smelt of stale urine. I had the place to myself, which was fortunate, as it could not have accommodated more than two or three people at a time. I used the slab urinal, then washed my hands, choosing the broken basin, so that the water splashed through the rim on to the floor. I laughed at this, then cursed as my trouser leg got splashed. But my anger didn't last long. I was in a mood of growing elation.

THE CANONGATE STRANGLER

I re-entered the low-ceilinged bar, pushing my way through the crowd, surrounded by working-class voices. There was no-one waiting for me, but I was not expecting anyone. Would I have another drink here or move on? I would have liked another one, but didn't want alcohol to impair the night's main business. Such restraint didn't come easily, but the incentive was strong. Besides, the pickings here were poor – all the women were with men or in groups – and the barmaid was calling for last orders. It was time to look for a place with a more promising selection, preferably with an even later licence.

I had somewhere in mind, but first decided to take a little air. I left the bar and found myself facing a river, with more buildings at the far side. I recognised it as the Water of Leith, not far upstream from its mouth, where it flowed into Leith Harbour; part of me seemed to have known this all along, while another part noticed it for the first time. I walked down to the bank, stepping over the low iron railing, and looked across. It was a clear, starry night and the moon was out. Facing me across the water was an old dock building, now stone-cleaned and revamped as a block of luxury flats. The old town of Leith, once a great seaport, now a run-down limb of the city itself, was in the process of being given a face lift, gap sites and derelict buildings mingling uneasily with new and refurbished developments as the area tried to drag itself up-market. "Well," I thought, laughing to myself, "I'll soon drag it back down again."

Only at this point did I fully realise what was happening: I had been asleep and dreaming, but not any more. My activated subconscious had been penetrated by the mind of the killer, sharpening the soft focus of the surreal into a deadly clarity, gradually rousing me from dream into nightmare.

There is a type of nightmare with which I am sometimes afflicted; I believe others have also experienced it, but it is by no means universal. In it, I believe myself to be awake and lying in bed. I attempt to get up, but find myself overcome by a great heaviness of body and am unable to move. Sometimes I think I have succeeded in leaving the bed, but this turns out to be a delusion, a dream within a dream; sometimes I make several such false attempts and become intensely frustrated. I may even realise that I am still asleep and try to rouse myself, but to no avail.

On the present occasion, I had similar feelings of panic and impotence. I knew that I was really at home, lying in my bed and that I should get up and do something to prevent the impending crime. And yet all attempts to rouse myself failed. My body remained fixed to the bed; at a vulnerable moment, the killer had plucked out my soul, leaving behind a piece of inert clay.

My resistance began to weaken, and then ended, first of all as I despaired of success and then, God help me, as I became infected by his mood.

He lit a cigarette and walked along the waterfront as he smoked; I am a non-smoker, and found I was enjoying the unaccustomed sensation as he drew the smoke into his lungs. It helped curb his impatience a little, but only for a short time. Finally, he went back to the road and walked quickly back the way he had come. Soon he found himself before a brightly-lit frontage, the only sign of life in a dark block. It was a focal point to which other people were drifting. Loud rock music issued from the open door.

I tried to walk in, but my way was barred by a large man in a flashy suit. "Five pounds entrance," he said.

"A fiver?" I protested. "I only want to dance, not buy the fuckin' place."

"That's the charge. Want to make something of it?"

"No no, pal. No offence. When does your bar close?"

"Three o'clock."

"You've talked me into it!" I paid him the money and proceeded inside.

After the comparatively bright lighting of the foyer, it took my eyes a moment or so to adjust to the gloom. The place was depressingly similar to every other disco I had known, probably to every other disco in the world: moving, coloured spotlights, deafening music, a pervasive, sickly odour that was a blend of aftershave and cheap perfume. A moderate number of people gyrated on the dance floor, but the real rush would come when the last pubs emptied.

I went up to the bar, which occupied the full length of one wall, waved over a barman and shouted an order. I only bought a beer, resisting, with an effort, my impulse to move on to spirits; with any luck there would be time for that later. My decision was reinforced when I heard the price.

I took a few gulps from my pint, then stood with my back to the bar, surveying the field. The music stopped, the disc jockey gabbled incoherently into an overloaded microphone, and another record began. The couples on the floor re-arranged themselves, some remaining there, others leaving, new ones moving in from the side of the hall. I began to work out which women were with boyfriends, which with female friends, and looked for any on their own; few would have arrived that way, but some might end up so, if their friends found partners.

The influx of people gradually increased and reached a peak. By this time my drink was almost finished, but I resisted the temptation to buy another and nursed the remaining dregs as I completed my survey.

Soon I had picked out a promising subject, a girl of about nineteen or twenty. She was pretty, in an ordinary sort of way, slightly on the plump side, though not excessively so, and she wore a green, low-cut dress. She had danced with several partners, but never the same one twice, and if she'd arrived with company, it had long since gone or become preoccupied. She had sat out the last dance on her own, and several times had looked at her watch. Once she smiled across at me and I smiled back. It was time to act.

"You took your time," she said.

"I'm shy."

"You don't look shy to me. You've had long enough to get over it."

"Don't you like older men?"

"Depends on the man."

This exchange was conducted in the usual disco fashion,

shouted in each other's ear between bouts of dancing. We proceeded in this way for two dances, and then we moved over to the bar and I bought her a drink. Here conversation was not much easier, but I eventually established that her name was Anne-Marie Colvin, that she worked in a local bakery and that she lived in Leith, only a few hundred yards away. No doubt she felt safe on her own, with her home being so near. I told her that I was a bus driver, that I came from Glasgow though I now lived in Edinburgh, and that I was divorced – it had not taken her long to enquire about my marital status. I called myself James Montgomery, after the officer in charge of the strangler investigation.

Eventually, I suggested that we go outside for a while.

"You work fast," she said. "I want to dance some more."

"We can do that later."

"I've only had one drink and a couple of dances. What do you think that entitles you to?"

"A breath of fresh air and a chat," I said. "Away from this din, where we can hear each other. We can go back in later."

She didn't take much more persuading. I had at least secured her interest, and was the only thing standing between her and an early night. We made our way to the door. "I'll need to get my coat," she said.

"I'll see you outside."

I went out to the vestibule and approached the doorman. "Is it all right if I go out for a while?"

"You're over 21, you can go out for the whole night."

"I mean, can I get back in again?"

"As long as you've got your ticket."

"Thanks."

I needed to go to the toilet, but didn't want to risk meeting her on the way out. With any luck, the doorman would remember that I left alone. I went out the front door and walked back up the block for a few yards, until I was clear of the disco frontage. Then I urinated against the wall, leaning my head against the brick so that I would look like a drunk. A couple of people passed me, but seemed to pay me no attention. I finished and lit a cigarette as I waited for her.

She came out the door of the disco, looking about her in either direction. She was now wearing a coat, made from imitation, fluffy fur. "Over here," I called, not too loudly.

"I thought you'd done a runner."

"Not me. Want a fag?"

"Thanks." I gave her a light and she took a draw. Then she looked down and took a step back.

"Oh no, someone's been having a pee here!"

"So they have," I said. "You get some dirty bastards about."

We moved away a few yards. She giggled. "Are you one of them?"

"It wasnae me. Honest."

"You know fine what I mean."

"I'm a gentleman," I said.

"Well that makes a change. There arenae many of you left."

We finished our cigarettes, and I led her away along the waterfront. We arrived at a bridge and took a right turn, across the river. She made no resistance as I put my arm around her, the soft, fluffy coat with the warm body beneath fitting comfortably to my side.

"Aren't you cold without a coat?"

"I've got you to keep me warm."

"Cheeky! Where are we going?"

"Just for a walk along the river."

At the end of the bridge we turned back along the waterfront, walking along the quay on the opposite side from the disco. A little further down, the quay narrowed to a walkway, which we approached through an entrance flanked by twin stone columns.

I began to lead her through it, but she hesitated.

"Are you sure we can go in here? It looks like private property."

"Who cares?"

"I don't want to trespass."

"Who's here to stop us? Anyway, it isn't private. Look at that." I pointed to a metal plaque on one of the columns. By the light of the nearest street lamp, we could just about make out the gold lettering. It told us that we were entering the Water of Leith Walkway, and gave the date when it had been opened by the Lord Provost of Edinburgh.

She relented and we went through the entrance. Now the river was fronted by a new block of flats, built in traditional style, part of the local renovation process. I began to understand her hesitancy; the footpath was not private, but the area seemed too up-market for her to feel at home. Of course, this only made me all the more determined to go there. At the end of the block, the walkway took a left turn where the river widened at the entrance of a tributary. The flats, fronted by the walkway, continued on for a few hundred yards. We rounded the corner, walked a little further on and then stopped. There was no-one else in sight. We were alone.

I turned her to face me, and kissed her gently. She responded positively, putting her arms around my neck and squirming against my body. We continued in that fashion for some time, then stopped for breath.

"You know, you're takin' a chance," I said.

"What do you mean?"

"It's quiet here. You don't know me. For all you know, I could be the strangler."

"Don't be daft. He only operates up in the city. In the posh areas."

"This is a posh area now. Anyway, the police are looking for him there. Maybe he's changed his pitch."

"I wish you wouldn't talk like that." She looked at me uncertainly, but I smiled at her, and she smiled back and relaxed again. "You don't look like the stranglin' type to me."

"How do you know?"

"I can tell."

"Woman's intuition?"

"That's it."

I took her head gently between my hands, pulled her face

towards mine and pecked her lightly on the lips, like the first soft kiss in a romantic film. "I never thought much of woman's intuition," I said, as I quickly slid my thumbs down to her throat and pressed hard.

She was so taken by surprise that she hardly struggled at all, her strength already waning by the time she realised what was happening. It made things less interesting, but at least I was spared some of the damage I had suffered the previous time.

When I was sure she was dead, I let her go and looked around me. There was still no-one about and the curtained windows of the flats stared blindly out. I had not made much noise, at least not enough to wake the sleepers above from their well-heeled slumber. I opened her handbag, removed her purse and pocketed its contents. There was twenty-four pounds in total, more than enough to cover my high expenses for the night's work. Then I dragged her over to the railing bordering the footpath and pushed the body under the chains that linked the metal posts. I gave her a further push and she rolled down the cobbled embankment into the water. I paused for a moment to see if anyone had heard the splash, but everything remained quiet. I looked over the railing. In the dim light from a nearby streetlamp, I could see her floating face down, her fluffy coat spreading out in the water, giving her the appearance of a huge jellyfish. I lifted her handbag, replaced the empty purse in it and took aim for her head. "Bullseye!" I muttered to myself as it made contact.

I went back along the walkway feeling considerably pleased with myself. Getting to know my victim first had made a pleasant change, added a personal touch. I looked at my watch. Ten past two. Plenty of drinking time left. I returned to the disco, showed my ticket at the door and found a corner at the bar.

I bought a double whisky and a half pint of beer, soon replacing the spirits with another double. I began to relax. I bought another drink and before long the music began to seem less intrusive. After a while, I fancied that the spotlights were less bright and the gloom was deepening. The image of the bar slowly faded into blackness. Had I fainted? I still seemed to be conscious.

I opened my eyes. I was at home in bed, back in the New Town, my wife lying beside me. For a moment or so I still felt drunk and then my head cleared. It took me a little longer to fully establish my separate identity, to pull it back out of the abyss which had swallowed it whole.

I looked at the bedside clock. A quarter to three. Jean appeared to be asleep, undisturbed by my mental excursion. My feelings were now in neutral gear, having disengaged from those of the killer, but as yet free of any replacement emotions of my own. These would come soon enough.

If I telephoned the police now, could they catch him before he left the disco? It was possible. But who would they look for? I was still unable to describe him. A man of indeterminate age, calling himself after Detective Chief Superintendant Montgomery?

There didn't seem much point in calling.

I went to the toilet, checked on the children and returned to bed. Jean was still asleep. It wasn't long before I joined her.

Presently, I dreamed that I was in a bar somewhere, with my wife sitting by my side. "I'm glad you brought me here Ted," she said. "You don't look like the strangling type to me."

"How do you know?" I asked her. "Take a look in Leith Harbour, then you'll see."

"There's always rubbish floating about down there," she said. "You're not the strangling type, I can tell. Call it a wife's intuition."

We sat in silence, taking comfort from one another's closeness.

EIGHT

IT DID NOT EVEN OCCUR TO ME to wonder if the murder would be reported in the news; I felt that to be as inevitable as the inclusion of the weather forecast. But I was wrong.

There was nothing on the breakfast bulletins, either on radio or TV, national or local. That seemed odd, because the strangler was now national news. I told myself that the body would not have been found until morning, that the report had not arrived in time. But there was nothing at lunchtime either, or in the evening, or all day on Sunday. Jean made a passing comment on my sudden obsession with current affairs, but thankfully did not persist with the subject.

Could the body have remained undiscovered for so long? It might have been drawn downstream by the current, but the river flowed into an enclosed harbour and it was unlikely to have been washed out to sea. Of course, I told myself, her waterlogged clothes would probably have caused the body to sink; perhaps it would surface weeks later, as the gases of decomposition rendered it buoyant – a nice, time-delayed present, courtesy of the strangler.

But surely by now she should have been reported missing? In a city with a killer at large, parents and friends were unlikely to be casual about an overnight disappearance. If it had been known that she was going to that particular disco, they should already have been dragging the river and harbour.

There could, of course, have been many explanations for

the delay. I could easily have thought of several. But I didn't want to.

Instead, I became obsessed by a single question: had it been a dream after all? Had my mind been so infected by the killer's lusts that it had begun to manufacture killings of its own? Had the whole episode been a fantasy indulgence in my latent homicidal tendencies, for which I had now found an ideal scapegoat in the person of the unknown killer?

Distasteful though this idea was, I clung to it desperately. It was preferable to the murder being real: better an imaginary killing of my own than an actual one by someone else. It helped keep at bay my self-disgust at the feelings the killer had awakened in me.

And yet it had not seemed like a dream, not the latter half of the experience. The last wisp of fantasy had blown away as I stepped out into that cold moonlight by the river. The incident had borne too much resemblance to my first nocturnal jaunt with the killer.

By Monday morning, when there was still no news, I was at the peak of my quandary. I had to settle the question permanently. It did not matter that the first two murders were definitely real, as were the others that he was bound to commit in the future. If I could get absolution for even one crime, then I was determined to grasp it.

How could I check? Telephone the police? I was still smarting from my last encounter, and how would they react to my latest story when there was not even a body? It didn't take me long to rule out that option.

I could perhaps check whether or not the victim had actually existed. She had given the killer her name. What was it again? It had been a two part Christian name. Mary Jane —? Mary Anne —? Ann-Marie, that was it! And her surname? It began with a 'C'. Colville? Calvin? That name gave me a further *frisson* of guilt, but it was not the one. It was near, though.

Colvin! Ann-Marie Colvin!

That didn't seem like too common a surname, and I

thought that my task was going to be easy until I looked up the Edinburgh telephone directory and found about two dozen of them. However, a cross-check with a street directory gave only two addresses in Leith, only one in the same area as the disco. Either that was it, or she was not on the telephone.

Or else she had never existed.

By this time I was due to leave for work. I had told Jean that I was checking the address of a client, but any further delay would have made her suspicious. I reflected briefly that, only a couple of months before, we'd had no secrets from each other.

In the office, I ignored my mail and stared at the telephone. Valerie came in, expecting dictation, and I sent her away again. I remained mesmerised for some minutes, then made up my mind and asked the telephonist for a line.

As the Leith number rang out, I still had no idea what I would say to the person who answered. "Is Ann-Marie there? —' Oh, she didn't come home on Friday night? There's a strangler in town you know, maybe you should check the harbour." Perhaps something more tactful would be better, but what? Who would I say I was? As the number continued to ring out, I several times resisted a strong urge to hang up and leave it be.

There was no reply. After a moment's hesitation, I tried again, in case I had dialled the wrong number. The result was the same. Mingled with my frustration was a certain feeling of relief. I called Valerie back in.

"Is there a copy of the Valuation Roll in the office?"

"Yes, I think so."

"Bring me the volume for Leith. And an Edinburgh street map."

"There's a street map in your bookcase."

"All right then, bring me it."

"What about your mail?"

"Never mind about that, we'll do it later."

The Valuation Roll was arranged in alphabetical order, but according to streets rather than names. I laboriously made my way through the volume, checking the list of occupiers for the name Colvin. By referring to the street map, I was able to skip those streets which seemed too far from the required area. I reached the end of the volume and then went through it again. Twenty minutes after I started, I had confirmed that there was still only one candidate: the one I had originally obtained from the phone book.

"Did you find what you wanted?" Valerie asked me when I had summoned her in again.

"Yes thanks."

She seemed on the point of asking me what it was all about, but realised that I didn't want to discuss it. "Do you want to do your mail now?"

"No, I think I'll go home."

"Why, is something the matter?"

"I don't feel well. I've got a dreadful headache. Could you cancel all my appointments? And don't ring me at home unless it's really urgent."

"Will you be in tomorrow?"

"I imagine so. If not, I'll phone you first thing."

By this time I had my coat on and was making for the door. Valerie seemed a little taken aback – none of this behaviour was typical of me – but she didn't argue. In truth, I could ill afford the time off, but I knew I would be unable to concentrate on my work until I had resolved my obsession.

It was a fine spring morning, quite inappropriate to the black mood which had enveloped me. I made my way through the old town, heading roughly north-west, until I saw a taxi that was for hire. I hailed it and asked the driver to take me to Leith.

As we got stuck in traffic on the South Bridge, I found myself looking down the Cowgate, towards the site of my second— *his* second murder. *That* killing had been real enough. Was there really any hope that the latest one could prove to be a fantasy?

I got the taxi driver to drop me in Leith town centre, a pleasant triangle of stonecleaned Victorian buildings, presided over by the statue of Robert Burns. Consulting my map, I saw that the address I sought was only a few streets away. Within a few minutes I had found it, an old tenement building in a street which the clean-up process had not yet reached. I went up the stairs, checking the names on the doors. The stairway smelt of dampness and old plaster, the stairs were worn and had not been cleaned for a long time, and it seemed arguable whether the last redecoration had been within the lifetimes of the present inhabitants. On the first half-landing, a window looked out on to a back court that was a wilderness of weeds and rubble. I found the house I was looking for on the second floor. It had a new, freshly-painted door, with a letter box of polished chrome, a lone attempt to reclaim some respectability from the surroundings. After only a moment's hesitation, I rang the doorbell. I still had no idea what I might say to the occupant, and prepared myself for some hasty improvisation. After waiting a couple of minutes, I rang the bell again.

There was no reply.

I tried a third time, then turned to the flat opposite and knocked on the door. There was no answer there either. I briefly thought of trying some other houses, then my nerve failed me and I hurried back out to the street.

There were other ways of checking my dream's authenticity. I retraced my steps to the town centre and, a hundred yards further on, arrived at the waterfront. Soon I had found the disco, in exactly the position that I remembered it. Naturally, it was closed. There were several pubs facing the river but one of them, with a low, old-fashioned frontage, seemed more familiar than the others. It too was closed. It was only 10.25. Another thirty-five minutes until opening time.

So far, nothing was proved. I had been in the area often enough in the past and knew its main landmarks. I had probably seen the pub before, probably even the disco, though I couldn't be sure. But I was certain of one thing. I had never been through the door of either. The other night's dream had been my only possible experience of their interiors.

For the moment there was no way to check further on this, so I made my way across the bridge, retracing the killer's journey with his victim. Across the river, I could already see the block of new flats, exactly in the position that I remembered them. Apart from the other night, had I been down this way since they were built? Did I know of their existence? I couldn't remember.

My spirits dropped as I passed through the twin stone columns, saw the metal plaque on one of them. Soon I was standing on the site of the murder, every step of the journey having been totally familiar. I looked over the railing, half expecting to see the large, furry jellyfish still floating there. But there was nothing, only an empty stretch of water. By daylight it was opaque and had lost much of its lustre. Anything could lie hidden in these dark waters.

This was not leading to the conclusion I wanted. I searched the ground nearby, looking for evidence of the struggle, for some other clue, but there was nothing.

I continued along the walkway until it diverged from the river, checking every visible inch of the water. Then I went back, recrossed the bridge, and made my way down the other bank, continuing my search. I found nothing, of course. If the body had been visible, someone else would have found it by now.

Shortly after 11 o'clock I went into the pub.

I bought myself a whisky and stood at the corner of the L-shaped bar, surveying the place. So far, I was the only customer. The pub was old-fashioned in style, with a low ceiling, leather-backed seats and wood-panelled walls. It didn't seem familiar, but the pub I remembered had been full of people and I'd only had a brief glimpse of it. So far I had seen nothing conclusive, though nothing inconsistent with my dream.

Four people came into the bar, three young women and a man. They spoke loudly and roughly, especially the women, and still seemed to be drunk from some late night celebration. They were known to the bar staff and they looked at me a little curiously, as though I was not quite the sort of fellow-customer they were used to. As I drank my whisky and listened to their raucous tones and loud laughter, I began, absurdly, to feel a little threatened; if the strangler had met one of these, I thought, he might have been the one to end up in the river. Obviously the transformation of the area still had some way to go. The fabric was proving easier to upgrade than the inhabitants.

I finished off my whisky and called to the barmaid. "Could you tell me where the Gents is please?"

"It's over there, just beside the fruit machine."

"Thanks."

I went in the direction indicated, past the gambling machine, standing unattended, its coloured lights flashing as it waited for its first victim. I opened a door with a frosted-glass panel and entered a small toilet with walls of dirty plaster and cracked tile. I saw two tiny wash basins, one with a bowl that had been smashed, leaving only a rim with a jagged edge—

It was more than just a feeling of déjà vu. Every detail of that dirty little lavatory precisely matched my memory from the other night. I looked in the WC, at the seatless bowl and exposed brickwork, then used the slab urinal and left the place.

As I went out the front door, I thought I heard one of the women make some comment about me, but I could not make out what it was.

I could not maintain my self-deception any longer. The third murder had been sufficiently corroborated. Somewhere in that river the strangler's latest victim lay hidden. She had not been found because, for some reason, she had not yet been missed.

Was there anything I could do? The police were unlikely to check the harbour on the basis of my story; if they did, and found the body, they would probably suspect me. In any case, it was too late to save her. It was better to leave things be.

The *next* victim, that was the one I had to think of. If I did everything in my power to save *her*, I might yet redeem myself. Since I still had no clue as to the killer's identity, I would have to wait until our next mental contact. On past form, that would only be when he was ready to strike again. I could only hope that, when he did, I would be awake and in a position to actively intervene.

What should I do now? I could not face going back to the

office, and if I went home, Jean's suspicions would undoubtedly be aroused. I felt like another drink, so I went into another pub. There were plenty to choose from.

This seemed to be a higher class of establishment than the one I had just left; at any rate, my entrance excited no curiosity from the sparse clientele. It was a long narrow bar, with a wider, raised area at the back. It had a dartboard and a television that was silently showing a schools programme. On the bar were several handpumps for dispensing traditional ales and a perspex case containing sandwiches and other, more substantial meals that could be cooked by microwave oven. I thought of buying a meal, but found I had no appetite. Instead, I bought another whisky and, as an afterthought, a half pint of the cask beer.

I sat on a stool at the bar, nursed my drinks, and stared across at the gantry. On one area of wall there had been pinned a number of postcards, presumably sent by customers on holiday; some had sea views, others rude cartoons. There were also a number of little notices, of the type often seen in bars. PLEASE DO NOT ASK FOR CREDIT, AS A SMACK ON THE MOUTH OFTEN OFFENDS. YOU DON'T HAVE TO BE MAD TO WORK HERE, BUT IT SURE HELPS. Did the management *really* imagine that these were in any way original? There was another which I had not seen before. THE LEITH POLICE DISMISSETH US, BUT ONLY AFTER CLOSING TIME. At another time I might have laughed, but not in my present mood.

I finished my drinks and bought others. The barman seemed to think that I was worth cultivating – a good omen for the upgrading process – and made several attempts to engage me in conversation. I didn't encourage him and he eventually gave up. I concentrated on getting drunk and trying to forget about the killings. In the former I succeeded admirably; the latter I did not manage, though I was able to dull the pain a little.

I left the pub after my second round of drinks. It was still only twelve o'clock and the sun seemed unnaturally bright, as if I were seeing everything in technicolor. I gradually made my way back towards the city centre, sampling further pubs at random.

By the time I reached the foot of Leith Walk, at the border between Leith and Edinburgh proper, I had been in another four pubs. I went into a fifth.

The barman, once he had got a proper look at me, regarded me in an unfriendly fashion. I was unused to so much drink on an empty stomach and had grown less cultivatable as my journey progressed. "A whisky and a half pint of heavy," I asked.

"I'm sorry mate, I think you've had enough."

"What?"

"I said, I think you've had enough."

"What the fuck do you mean? I want a whisky and a half—"

"You're getting nothing here. I think you should go."

I grabbed the barman by the collar and hauled him half across the counter. With my free hand, I lifted an empty pint tumbler, smashed it on the edge of the counter and held it to the barman's throat. "Are you going to get that order?"

I was bigger and younger than him, but he was sober. He thrust me back, and I staggered and fell to the floor, the remains of the tumbler smashing around me. A babble of voices arose.

"Jesus Christ!"

"Vicious bastard."

"Phone the police."

"Well dressed, too. Who the hell does he think he is?"

I tried to get up. Someone said, "Bastard!", kicked me and I fell back down again.

"He's calling the police."

"Too bloody right."

The fact that I was in danger somehow penetrated the clouds of alcohol. I managed to regain my feet and ran for the door. No-one stopped me.

Outside, everything was normal. The afternoon sun still shone and the streets were full of people. At the crossroads, the statue of Queen Victoria, guarding the front entrance of

Woolworths, looked down at me unamused. Was any other city so appropriately landmarked by statues? In the middle of the wide thoroughfare was a taxi rank. I went over to the cab at the head of the queue and got in.

The driver seemed unsure of me, but relented when he saw the contents of my wallet. Soon I was home.

Fortunately, Jean and the children were out and didn't witness my arrival. I undressed and went straight to bed.

NINE

I THINK THE KILLER must have resented not receiving the credit due him for his latest crime. By Wednesday of the same week, as the body remained undiscovered, he decided to reaffirm his presence. But before that I had to pay the price for my Monday escapade.

I think it was mentioned earlier that I am not a very heavy drinker; the reader may find this difficult to believe, but before the onset of the extraordinary events that I am presently recording, it was in fact true. Like many people, I got into a few drunken episodes as a youth, but since then, particularly since my marriage, I have only taken alcohol occasionally and in moderate quantities. In other words, I had been completely out of training for a pub crawl and suffered as a result.

I am not sure when Jean arrived home that afternoon. It may be that she found me earlier and allowed me to sleep on, or perhaps she didn't immediately notice that I was home before my usual time; at any rate, she looked in on me shortly after I awoke, around seven o'clock. I told her that I was feeling ill, that I had left the office early because of it, and that I still couldn't face having anything to eat. She didn't argue and left me alone again. She said very little in fact. The barrier between us was strengthening.

By that time my illness was not feigned. Why had I taken so much whisky? My usual drink, on the few occasions when I did indulge, was gin. I had not drunk whisky for years, ever since a disastrous youthful experiment which had conditioned

70

me permanently against it. Since then, the very thought of the stuff has made me feel ill.

This memory triggered a response and I had to make my way quickly to the bathroom for a bout of retching, which carried on long after there was nothing left in my stomach to disgorge. I returned to bed with watering eyes and a tight knot of pain in my stomach. Luckily my family all seemed to be downstairs at the time.

The killer, I remembered, had been drinking whisky at the disco the other night. It had been his way of relaxing after a good night's murder and robbery.

I was still slightly drunk when I awoke, and as the evening progressed and I sobered up further, my condition grew gradually worse. For the time being I was unable to get back to sleep, my Puritan subconscious having decided that I should stay awake and suffer. I lay in bed feeling wretched, with no company but my thoughts. They did not provide good companionship.

One thing I had forgotten about hangovers was the amount of mental activity they seem to generate. I am not sure whether this is a direct effect of the alcohol, or whether the brain is merely goaded into extra work by the body's incapacity, but the phenomenon is real enough. Another accompaniment to a hangover, I rediscovered, is a mood of intense depression.

I experienced both of these consequences in full. Over and over again, I relived the killer's crimes and felt the remorse that should rightfully have been his. This was accompanied by a repeated resolve that I would do everything in my power to stop his next murder.

Almost as harrowing as my memory of the murders was my blurred recollection of the incident in that last pub. Did it really happen? Or was it a just a drunken nightmare from the period when I was sleeping off my binge? I hoped so, but wasn't convinced. I was in a mood to believe the worst. If it was indeed true, then my behaviour was frightening. It was not the way a respectable lawyer was supposed to carry on; it was something he tried to explain away to unconvinced judges on behalf of his clients. And what if one of my clients had witnessed the episode?

But my main concern was not the affront to my professional dignity or the fear of being found out. It was the innate aggression it had revealed within me. I couldn't remember ever having behaved in such a way before, not even in the days of my wild youth. Had this trait always been buried in me, or was it a recent acquisition?

As if my conscience was not overworked enough, I also found my mind frequently returning to the office and my neglected business. Little tasks that I would have dispatched with hardly a thought while sitting behind my desk, grew into enormous problems as I lay in bed powerless to do anything about them. I began to worry if I would be well enough to return to work the following day. This almost became a self-fulfilling prophecy as these and other thoughts continued to keep me awake, long after Jean had joined me.

I would have felt the better for another day off work, but forced myself to go in. Soon I was back in the thick of it, struggling with Valerie's help through two days of accumulated mail. Luckily, I had no court appearances and had a rare opportunity to catch up with some deskwork. All the same, I found it hard going.

Valerie became concerned about me. "Are you sure you're all right, Mr. Middleton? You look a bit pale."

I had just finished my dictation, and the unusual concentration required had left me with a severe headache. "I don't feel very well Valerie. I think I came back too soon."

"Can I get you anything?"

"A couple of aspirins maybe. And a glass of water."

She brought me them, and after a short rest I began to feel a little better. "Right," I said. "What else have I got on?"

"No appointments until the afternoon. Oh, and Mr. Wintergreen wanted to see you."

"Oh yes, I wonder what he wants?" Normally I tried to avoid an audience with my senior partner because of the time it tended to waste. The art of précis was one that tended to elude him. But on this occasion it would be better to get the meeting over with while I was still incapable of doing anything more productive. I phoned his secretary, learned that he was free to see me and sent Valerie away to type the letters I had dictated.

As befitted the senior partner and co-founder of the firm, Andrew Wintergreen occupied the most opulent suite in our Victorian office building. He matched his surroundings well, with his expensive business suit and silver hair. He was less active in the firm than he had once been, though his current function was more than just window dressing. He made me welcome in his usual dignified, paternal fashion.

"Come in Ted. Have a seat."

"Thanks."

"Cigarette?"

"Yes thanks." I took a cigarette from the box he held out to me, put it in my mouth and leaned over his desk to accept a light. Then I stopped and took it out of my mouth again. "I'm sorry, I don't smoke."

"Of course you don't. Silly of me."

It was typical of him to forget that I was a non-smoker, but it was something I usually remembered myself. He made no move to accept the cigarette back, so I put it down on his desk, feeling a little awkward. He replaced the box in his drawer. He didn't smoke either and only kept the cigarettes for visitors.

"Well Ted," he said. "It's nice to see you. How are you?"

"Still a bit fragile."

"Good, good. You're looking well. Still keeping you busy, are we?"

"Can't complain."

"I know. It never stops, never stops." He hesitated.

"Was there something you wanted to see me about?" I asked.

"Ah yes, I was looking for you yesterday. I think you were in court or something."

"I went home. I wasn't feeling very well."

"Really? Are you all right now?"

"Not too bad."

"Good, good." He hesitated again. "And you're keeping busy?"

"Yes. Was there some work you wanted to give me?"

"No, no. I just wondered— "

I felt an impulse to lean across his desk and shake him violently until he got to the point. I checked myself, of course. My hangover seemed to be getting to me. It was quite normal for my senior partner to circle endlessly round a subject before eventually tackling it. I liked him well enough and generally put up with his circumlocutions without too much impatience; usually I managed to keep out of his way altogether.

He paused again, apparently experiencing difficulty in finding the right words for what he wanted to say. I recognised the symptoms. The amount of tact required for his message had stopped it from emerging at all. Had I done something wrong? My well-exercised conscience sprang back into life, conjuring up imaginary offences.

"You're a very good lawyer, Ted," he said finally.

"I do my best."

"Yes, you work very hard, very hard. You get through a lot of business."

"Have I done something wrong?"

"No no no — No, of course not. You make a lot of money for the firm. You bring in a lot of work. I'm not complaining, not complaining at all. Certainly not. It's just that, I sometimes feel, just a little, it's only a small thing, but with the greatest respect— "

For God's sake, I thought, my impatience rising again as his point got buried in endless qualifications. "There is something wrong," I said aloud.

"Not at all. Not at all. It's only that, well, some of your clients — not all of them, most of them are excellent people, excellent — but one or two of them, in the nicest possible way, I mean— "

I began to detect the message that was hidden in the protective verbiage. "You mean my legal aid clients?"

"Ah — Yes. Exactly. Mind you, I've got nothing against

them, but — "

"Have they been causing any trouble?"

"Oh no, not at all. Only — Well, we are a very respectable firm you know. Some of our clients are quite well off, quite influential in some cases. You know Hector Menzies? Yes of course you do. Well only the other day he was in to see me and while he was in the waiting room, there was, well — I've nothing against these people, you know, nothing at all."

His point was now absolutely clear. The middle-class bedrock of Summers & Wintergreen's clients didn't like having to mix with the criminals and other unfortunates who came to me for help.

"You want me to stop doing legal aid work?"

"Oh, no no. You've built up a good court practice. Very high turnover of business. You bring in a lot of money. But, with respect, I mean— "

Eventually I got the full story. Summers & Wintergreen needed to have a court practice to serve their existing clients – even the most solid citizens, after all, sometimes got divorced or drove with too much to drink. And, though we were an established firm, we were not exactly one of the largest in the city, and so a legal aid practice brought extra income, courtesy of the taxpayer, that was very welcome in these competitive times. It was just that the appearance of some of the people it brought into the office could cause distress to the other clients. Luckily, however, near my office there was an old store that could easily be converted into a separate waiting-room. The two lots of clients might still occasionally collide in the hallway or in the street outside, but that was a small price to pay in the cause of profit and social justice.

I appreciated his point – once, that is, I had managed to extract it from the diplomatic meanderings in which it was almost smothered – and yet for some reason it made me very angry. If my clients were second-class citizens, this reflected on me as well. And on what basis did I decide who to segregate? What should I do if the good Hector Menzies came to see me because he had driven after too many gins and got

breathalysed? Dump him in with the burglars and drug addicts?
I didn't think that was the intention.

I kept these thoughts to myself and told Andrew
Wintergreen that I was happy with his proposal. However, I
mentioned it to Valerie when she came in with my mail to sign.

"What do you think of my clients, Valerie? Are they good
enough for you?"

"I don't understand."

"Mr. Wintergreen wants to keep them separate from the
other clients. We're going to convert the old store into a special
waiting-room."

"Well— " She hesitated, trying to sound out my mood.
"Maybe it wouldn't be such a bad idea."

"Really? You surprise me, Valerie. I didn't think you were
a snob."

She coloured. "I'm not. I've got nothing against these
people, nothing at all, but— "

"You're beginning to sound like Mr. Wintergreen. Sorry,
that's not fair."

"I know what he means. Remember that man who came
in to see you on Friday? Mr. Coldstream?"

"The Grassmarket Flasher? What about him?"

"Well, he was sitting beside one of Mr. Wintergreen's
clients in the waiting room – Mr. Menzies I think it was –
and—"

"Don't tell me he showed Hector Menzies his wares?"

Valerie's colour deepened. "Really, Mr. Middleton. It's
just that, well, I don't think he has a bath very often."

I laughed. "So that's it. At all costs we must keep the
stinking rich away from the stinking poor. We'd better get an
extractor fan put in the new waiting room, so that we can blow
all the B.O. back out into the street."

She laughed, a little hesitantly. "I'm sorry, Valerie," I said.
"I'm still not quite myself. It's probably all for the best."

"Yes. Especially since — Well, there seem to have been
more of them recently."

I thought about this further after she had gone. Was my

legal aid work on the increase? More often than not the clients it brought in were seen by me in the court house or at the police station or in jail, and yet those who came to the office were still enough to create a problem. If it was only now causing bother, perhaps I *was* taking on more of them.

What was the reason, I wondered? Did I accept them simply because they turned up and I enjoyed the work? Or was I developing a social conscience?

TEN

ON THE EVENING of the following day, I was alone in my sitting-room, working on some legal papers. It was around 11 o'clock, the children were long since in bed and my wife had retired about twenty minutes before. As the room was at the back of the house, no traffic sounds could be heard and the silence was complete. This was my situation when I again felt my mind merge with that of the other man. I seemed to be simultaneously sitting indoors and walking along a city street, both sets of sensations reaching me with equal clarity. Once again I experienced with him that unique excitement as the scent of the kill reached our nostrils. As if I were preparing to watch a film, I got up and put out the light.

The illusion was now complete. I was walking eastwards, towards the end of Princes Street. I passed Register House and the Wellington Monument and turned downhill towards Leith Walk. There was still some traffic about and a few other pedestrians, though I saw no unaccompanied women. This did not worry the murderer, as his plan was already made.

So great a spell had the prospect of the adventure cast upon me, that for the moment I had forgotten my resolution. Then I remembered my duty: I was supposed to prevent the murder, not join in the fun. Masked by the feverish excitement of the hunt, the voice of my conscience sounded very faint. With an effort, I managed to fan the spark into a precarious flame. To help me distance myself, in an attempt to cling on to my separate identity, I got up and put on the light again. It took me some time, as I could see nothing of the room I was in, and at one point I banged my shins against a coffee table; also, every inch of the way, I was fighting against the mesmerising influence of the killer's lust. It was as if I were trying to wade into the sea against the overwhelming force of a tidal wave.

Eventually I succeeded and returned to my seat, moving this time with much less difficulty. The killer's mood still gripped me, but at least my own world had a visual claim upon my attention. I tried to build upon this and to work out some plan of action.

He intended to kill again, of that I could have no doubt. How could I stop him? While in the grip of his homicidal fever, it was almost impossible for me to think coherently, and conclusions that should have been obvious had to be eased from my unwilling brain through a maze of conflicting sensations.

There were two things I could do: I could try to intervene personally, or I could call the police.

With the the former of these, I faced the difficulty that the killer was at least a mile away from me. If I tried to drive my car, with two different sets of visual images coming at me through the windscreen, I would almost certainly cause an accident. But if I tried to overtake him on foot, with my vision equally impaired, I would never get to him on time, even supposing that I didn't get run over first.

If I phoned the police, what would I say? "There's a man walking down Leith Walk, officer. He's the Canongate Strangler and he's just about to kill again." "I see sir, and what does this man look like?" "I'm afraid I don't know." "How do you know where he is and that he's going to commit a murder?" "It's difficult to explain, officer. You see I'm in some sort of telepathic communicaton with him." "Really sir, that's very interesting. What did you say your name was again?" "Edward Middleton." "Oh yes sir, Superintendant Montgomery told us about you. You're that nutter that came in to see him after the last murder. Are you going to get off the line or do you want me to book you?"

I didn't call the police. In retrospect, I realise that there are flaws in the above argument. If I could have summoned the determination to make the call, it might well have gone along the lines I had imagined. But at least the call would have been recorded, and if the killing took place as predicted, I might have been believed in future. But I didn't think of this at the time.

In any case, it was my job to prevent the killing, not explain it afterwards. So what else could I do? If I could not handle a car myself, maybe someone else could drive me. I could wake Jean, but how could I persuade her in time that I was not crazy? Besides, I might be putting her in danger, and we could not leave the children unattended.

I could phone a taxi! I went to the hall, found the telephone book, and returned with it to the telephone extension in the sitting-room. I dialled one number and it was engaged. So was the second one I tried. The third could have sent a cab in fifteen minutes, but that might have been too late. All this time, the killer's footsteps pounded in my head like a migraine, his evil desires choking my brain, depriving it of rationality; now he was passing the St. James Centre, whose modern concrete outlines clashed garishly with its period surroundings, and was walking under the unsightly new footbridge that linked the Centre with the other side of the road. He continued downhill, all the time getting nearer to his goal. My vision continuing to blur with his, I dialled another taxi firm and got a wrong number. I would be quicker going outside and trying to hail one. I went back to the hall, with difficulty found my coat, went out the front door and began to walk the few hundred yards to the nearest main road. Before me there were two roads, two pavements, two sets of streetlights. My footsteps were out of synchronisation with his and I stumbled frequently; I became confused between my two pairs of legs and felt as if I were walking on an elastic surface. A man was walking towards the strangler, but the killer did not get out of his way; then I bumped into the man and realised that he was on my own street.

I apologised and carried on. Soon I reached the main road and looked up and down it for the yellow light of a Hackney cab. The lights of the other street swivelled round with my gaze, making me dizzy. I could see no sign of a cab. Then I saw one and tried to hail it. It drove past, and I realised it had been driving along the murderer's street and not my own.

Now the killer had passed the junction at the end of York Place and had entered Leith Walk proper. Was he returning to Leith to duplicate his last, undiscovered crime? No, he was nearing his destination. I stumbled back home and returned to my sitting-room.

There was one last way in which I might be able to intervene. After the second killing, I had briefly brought my presence to the murderer's notice. If I could do so again, if I could once more make the mental link a two-way one, perhaps I could persuade him to change his mind; if I could not appeal to his better nature, which seemed unlikely, I could at least make him aware that he was being observed, which might deter him.

I tried to project my mind into his, to call to him across the rooftops of the city. I walked over to the centre of the room, underneath the light, and stared into the naked bulb until the glare hurt my eyes, hoping I could flash some sort of beacon into the eyes of the other man. But he carried on, intent on his purpose, unaware of my weak signals. Our previous links had occurred when he was on an emotional high, and my only successful counter-attack had been when my revulsion had reached a similar degree of intensity. But now his passions were in dominance, and a mental door had been slammed on me, against which I could only scratch feebly.

There was nothing I could do. The tiny remaining spark of my conscience for a moment knew despair, then flickered and died. At first I was determined not to participate in his pleasure, and decided to leave the room light on. Then I got up and switched it off again. If I was about to witness a murder, I argued unconvincingly, I should observe as much as I could.

As I sat once more in the dark, the vision was again complete and free of interference. By now the murderer had passed the end of London Road and the intrusion of modern buildings upon this historic city was well behind him; his route, on either side, was flanked by older buildings, mostly blocks of flats. At street level, there were mainly shops and some pubs; the latter were about to close, but the main exodus had not yet occurred and the streets were fairly quiet. He had still not seen any unaccompanied women, but that did not deter him; he was cunning and knew where to look for fresh pickings. And by now, as his elation moved towards a peak, my resistance was dead and I was with him all the way. I was a boy again, I had regressed to the days of my wild youth and had thrown myself headlong into yet another forbidden scrape.

ELEVEN

SOON I stopped at a door between two shops. Above the door, a lighted notice said 'Samantha's Sauna.'

I entered and walked up a flight of stone stairs to the first floor landing. There I found a door marked 'Reception.' I went in.

I found myself facing a middle-aged woman behind a desk. Further inside, two younger women sat in a small lounge, boredly watching TV. The middle-aged woman gave me a professional smile of welcome. "Can I help you?"

"Yes," I said, "I'd like a massage."

"Half an hour?"

"That'll be fine."

"Do you want a sauna?"

"No."

"It doesn't cost any extra, but it's up to you. That'll be eight pounds please."

I paid her and she put the money in a box, inside her desk drawer. "What's your first name?"

"Albert. Albert DeSalvo."

I had given her the name of the notorious Boston Strangler but, as I had suspected, it seemed to ring no warning bell in her memory. This amused me considerably.

"Albert will do," she said. She wrote the Christian name in a book, along with my time of arrival, then gave me a large white towel and a locker key. She called over one of the girls. "Vicki!"

Vicki was an attractive blonde in her early twenties. She wore a tight-fitting, low-cut dress and black stockings held up by frilly suspenders, which were only partly concealed by her short skirt. She gave me a friendly smile which seemed sincere enough.

"This is Albert," said the older woman. "Will you take care of him?"

"Hello Albert," said the girl. "I'm Vicki. Have you been here before?"

"No."

"I'll show you around then. Just follow me."

She led me back out of the door, explaining that the sauna and massage rooms were on the floor above. We went further up the stone stairs and through another door. This led into a corridor, from which there opened several small, dimly-lit rooms. At the end of the corridor I saw the pinewood frontage of a sauna. Vicki allocated me a massage room and directed me to the locker room and showers.

"Are you having a sauna?" she asked.

"No, I don't think I'll bother."

"In that case, I'll hang on until you're ready."

The situation was working out as I had planned. At that time of night, in mid-week, I had reckoned the chances were high of being the only customer, and so it had turned out. The reception being on a separate floor was a bonus.

I undressed, left my clothes in my locker and took a shower. The water was tepid and the flow uneven. Obviously the showers were not the main attraction of this establishment nor, I suspected, was the sauna. I didn't wait long. Quickly drying myself, I wrapped the towel around me and returned to the massage room.

The small room was almost filled by the narrow massage table, whose cushioned top was covered by a broad roll of tissue paper, an easily replaceable bedsheet that bore no evidence of the previous occupants' activities. Pop music, low in volume, came from a speaker in the corner of the ceiling. Vicki locked the door behind me and got me to lie face down on the table, divesting me of my towel in the process. "There's no need to be shy," she assured me.

"I'm no' shy."

"Good. Would you like oil or powder?"

"Which do you suggest?"

"I think oil's more — sensuous," she said, hesitating meaningfully.

"I'll take oil then."

She began to apply oil to the back of my body in what she no doubt thought was an erotic manner. She returned frequently to the insides of my thighs, just below the buttocks. I had a feeling that she was not a qualified masseuse. While she continued this pretence of a massage, she tried to engage me in polite conversation.

"What do you do for a living, Albert?"

"I'm on the dole."

"Oh. I'm surprised you can afford places like this."

"I've got a bit put by. I can afford a fling now and then."

"Good. You'll have a good fling here."

"I'm sure I will."

"If you enjoy it enough, maybe we can persuade you to come back here for your next one."

"I wouldn't bank on it, but you never know."

We continued to talk inconsequentially. Then she asked me to turn over and for a short while rubbed oil into the front of my body, studiously missing my groin, though not by very much. Finally she said, "Would you like any extras, Albert?"

"What kind of extras?"

She laughed. "Haven't you been to a place like this before?"

"No."

"Don't you know the sort of thing we offer?"

"I've got an idea."

"You're not a policeman, are you?"

"Give us a break! Do I look like a cop?"

She regarded me appraisingly. "You're big enough, but no, I don't think so. You seem too nice."

"Thanks. You've no idea how nice."

"So do you want to know what's on the menu?"

"Yes please."

She recited a list of sexual services, each with its allocated price. I thought about it for a while then made my choice. I didn't worry about the cost, as I had no intention of paying her.

She undressed and took my place face up on the massage table. She wanted to leave on her stockings and suspenders, but I made her take them off as well; I had no need of such outdated erotic frills. I had elected to give her a massage before getting down to the main business. I put oil on my hands and gently caressed her legs, her groin, her stomach, her breasts. She had a lovely body. I was enjoying myself.

"You've got big strong hands."

"It's been noticed before."

The top end of the table was against the wall, so I had got her to lie with her head at the bottom. She had seemed surprised but, not knowing my reason, had complied readily enough. I was therefore able to work my way round to the end of the table until I was behind her head, looking down the length of her body.

"Do you think you can turn me on?" I asked her.

"I'm sure I can."

"I'm sure you can too."

"So what is it? What turns you on?"

I bent down until my mouth was only a few inches from her ear. "Stranglin' people," I said.

There was a pause while she took in my words. Then she gave a start and tried to sit up. "I don't think that's very fun—" Her escape and her protest were simultaneously stopped as I grabbed her by the throat.

"I wasnae jokin'," I said.

I had got her into a perfect position for the deed. Apart from an ineffectual attempt to loosen my grip with her fingers, she could do nothing, as I was out of her reach. I had been annoyed by the premature end of the last two murders; now I could enjoy her death at my leisure. Nor did I want to use a ligature when I could manage with my bare hands; I wanted the skin to skin contact, the direct tactile communication between killer and victim. Only thus could I squeeze the maximum satisfaction from my act.

As her life drained away beneath my fingers, I realised what little need I had of her sexual favours. No brief sordid coupling, no sad parody of the life-creating process could ever approach this experience. Her life force seemed to pass straight from her body to mine, and as she died I felt stronger, more vital than I had ever done. This was being alive! This was the meaning of existence!

When I had finished, I closed the door on the massage room and its contents. The upper floor was still empty, no other late customers having arrived to disturb my pleasure. It seemed unlikely that any would come now, and my half hour still wasn't up, so they wouldn't be expecting Vicki to reappear just yet. That gave me time to have another shower, to wash off the oil. I leisurely soaked myself in the tepid water, feeling not in the slightest hurry to leave.

I dried myself, then went to the toilet, a small WC near the sauna. Above the cistern was a plastic notice with a cartoon of a cute little boy and the following message:

If you sprinkle when you tinkle,
Please be sweet and wipe the seat.

I found this very amusing and laughed aloud as I deliberately pissed all over the seat.

I remembered that I had left my locker key in the massage room and went back to retrieve it, taking a last look at Vicki before I left. She lay ungracefully on the massage table, her darkened face and foam-flecked mouth twisted into the usual death-grimace. She no longer looked attractive, merely a used receptacle that had been cast aside.

Perhaps it was time for me to leave. I went back to the locker room, dressed quickly and then, in order to comb my hair, turned to a mirror on the wall beside the lockers.

My mind had become so united with that of the killer that at first I saw nothing in the mirror to remark upon. And then I,

Edward Middleton, regained enough of my separate identity to realise that, for the first time, I was looking at the face of the murderer.

And the face I saw was my own!

Until now, as far as I could tell, my communication with the other man had remained in one direction only. He had briefly become aware of me at the second murder, but so far I had no reason to believe that he knew of my presence on this occasion. However, it now seemed to me that the force of my shock reached back to him and our link again became a mutual one. I felt from his mind a surge of surprise, of anger at the intrusion, of curiosity as to my identity. I would also have expected some evidence of fear, but this seemed an emotion to which he was not noticeably subject.

He dismissed me contemptuously from his mind and made his way quickly out to the stairs. We passed the door to the reception without incident and were soon hurrying off up the street, back towards the city centre.

Suddenly the dark street seemed to fill with light, as if a set of floodlights had been switched on. For a few moments I was disoriented. Then I realised that my sitting room was once more superimposed upon the street. Someone had turned on the light.

It was Jean. "Ted, what on Earth's going on?"

"What?"

"Why are you sitting in the dark?"

"I — I must've fallen asleep."

"I heard you cry out. It woke me up and nearly scared me to death."

"I cannae remember. I musta been dreamin'."

Jean regarded me in a manner that was puzzled as well as worried. "Ted, why are you speaking like that?"

"Like wha'?"

"Your accent's changed."

I realised that I had been talking with a Glasgow accent, in the voice of the murderer! I corrected myself with an effort. "I hadn't noticed."

She sat down opposite me and continued to regard me with concern. I said nothing more. The silence grew more and more embarrassing, the barrier that had grown between us once more firmly in place.

Finally, she said, "Ted, it's time we talked about this."

"Talked about what? I fell asleep and had a bad dream, that's all."

"You've had a few bad dreams lately. On Friday night, you were gabbling like a maniac in your sleep. And what about that carry on at the Faculty Dinner? Or the small matter of missing your work on Monday and getting drunk instead?"

"What do you mean? I was ill."

"Come off it, the bedroom reeked of drink when I found you. And the state of your clothes! And I can recognise a hangover when I see one. What's got into you, Ted? You're not a drinker."

I said nothing. There seemed little point in further denials.

"There's no use continuing to pretend there's nothing wrong," she said. "Something's been bugging you for ages. You've lost weight, you're becoming irritable. Even the children are beginning to notice it. I think it's time you saw a doctor."

"A doctor? You mean a psychiatrist?"

"I mean your GP, to begin with. Then we'll see what he says."

"And you think he'll send me to a shrink?"

She sighed. "I didn't say that. But you'll need to do *something*."

"There's nothing any doctor can do."

"Why are you so sure?"

"I just know."

She exhaled in exasperation. "For God's sake!" Then she brought herself back under control and tried a last appeal. "Ted, we never used to have secrets. We used to trust each other. Why won't you let me help you?"

"There's nothing you can do."

She waited for a moment, looking for some reply, but I

said nothing. Then she sighed again and rose to her feet. "Have it your own way. I'm going back to bed." She left the room, banging the door behind her.

One of my major regrets now is my failure to take Jean into my confidence. She would have given me more strength to fight off the killer's seduction. But at the beginning, when confession would have been relatively easy, I had wanted to spare her the burden; now, although I had not personally laid a finger on any of the victims, I was afraid that my confession might alienate her completely. If she believed me, that is. If she didn't, she was likely to have me forcibly committed!

The gap between us was now too great to bridge. In any case, I could think of no way a doctor might help me, unless he was a witch doctor. Any hopes of a rational explanation of my situation had now disappeared and I was filled with a fear of the supernatural. I was being haunted by my double, an evil doppelganger who was committing hideous crimes in my image. How else could I account for that face in the mirror?

I had thought that my nightmare could not get worse. I now saw I had been wrong.

TWELVE

THIS LATEST INCIDENT demoralised me more than any of the others. My earlier theory was that I had discovered in myself some latent power of telepathy, of the ability to read minds. I knew that there were people who thought such things possible, though in the past I had never believed it myself. In recent weeks I had come to accept it as some kind of rational explanation upon which to cling. But now even this small comfort was denied me.

There followed several weeks of precarious normality. As before, it was to prove temporary. The strangler's position was now secure as a national celebrity, the latest victim's profession having given the affair a sordid glamour which the press were quick to exploit. However, for the time being I was spared any further mental contact with the killer, and as I once more picked up the pieces of my personal and professional life, I again began to take a more rational view of the matter. The killer had to be just another man, an evil one, but with human weaknesses and limitations. Apart from that one glance in the mirror, our brief contacts had revealed no evidence to the contrary. No other view was compatible with sanity. I became convinced that I had over-reacted, in a moment of stress, to a passing resemblance between us.

Now that there were witnesses who had seen the killer, a photofit picture appeared in the press, and this also helped reassure me. It bore no more likeness to me than to thousands of other men: the hair was longer, the style of dress unlike mine and I already knew that he spoke with a different accent. On the other hand, the surviving witnesses had seen the killer only briefly, and I knew from my professional experience how much their description was likely to be worth. But I didn't dwell on that aspect.

The first indication that this uneasy peace was about to end came a fortnight after the sauna killing. I had an appointment to see a petty criminal called Sammy Noakes, who had been arrested on a breaking and entering charge and was looking for a lawyer to defend him under the legal aid system. He was being held in the same police station as my embarrassing meeting with Chief Superintendant Montgomery. My business had taken me back there several times since, but entering the building still recalled to me the emotions I had felt on that day. Fortunately I didn't run into Montgomery, and in fact had not seen him since that first occasion.

In any case, such considerations soon became of minor importance. I had not acted for Noakes before and was now meeting him for the first time. I was taken to his cell by a policeman, who introduced me to the prisoner and then locked me in with him. Noakes was a small, thin, shabbily-dressed man in his early thirties. I took this much in as I moved towards him, with my hand extended, to introduce myself.

His reaction took me completely by surprise. As soon as he got a proper look at me, all the colour drained from his face, he began to tremble and his eyes widened in terror. He backed away from me until he had reached the far wall of the cell.

"Is something the matter?" I asked him.

I took a step towards him, and he flattened himself against the cell wall, as if he were trying to squeeze his body through the solid brick. "Keep away from me!" he said.

"I'm sorry," I said, not knowing how to react. "I was told that you wanted a lawyer." I gave him my name again.

"You're no lawyer!" he told me. "How did you get in here? What do you want?"

"I don't understand. You must have mistaken me for someone else."

"There's no mistake. I know you. Get out of here! Get away from me!"

His screaming had brought back the policeman. "Is everything all right?" he asked me.

"*I'm* all right," I said. "But I don't know what's got into him."

"Get rid of him!" shouted Noakes. "*He's* the one who should be in here, not me. He's no lawyer, he's tricked you. He's an evil bastard. Get him out of here before he kills me!" He sat down on his bunk and began to sob.

"I think you'd better let me out," I told the policeman.

He did as he was told and locked the door again behind me. "What's wrong?" he asked.

"God knows. He seems to have confused me with someone else. He thinks I'm an imposter."

"Would you like me to have a word with him?"

"I don't think it would do any good. You'd better get him another lawyer."

If the policeman thought it odd that I should give in so easily, he gave no indication as he showed me out. He grumbled a little about criminals who had no right to be so fussy, but made no attempt to change my decision.

In normal circumstances I might have persisted with trying to sort out the confusion. But I had no stomach for it. Noakes did not know it, but the incident had terrified me as much as him!

This episode certainly weakened my tottering defences, but it was merely a prelude to even greater attacks upon my morale. The next one occurred about a week later.

I had gone to the sheriff court for a criminal trial. I was in an ante-room putting on my gown when a solicitor I knew came in from the courtroom. He seemed surprised to see me. "Hullo, Ted," he said. "I didn't think you were on today?"

"Why not?"

"When I saw you earlier, I thought you must have the day off."

"What are you talking about? When did you see me?"

"Don't you remember? About ten minutes ago, in the public benches. I must say you've done a quick change. You weren't exactly dressed for court before."

"You must have made a mistake," I said. "I've only just arrived. Anyway, what would I be doing in the public benches?"

"That's what I wondered myself. Bit of a busman's holiday, coming here on your day off."

"I haven't got a day off. I've got a trial on."

"I can see that now." He was beginning to get a little exasperated, as if I was accusing him of being a liar or a fool. "But that's not what it looked like ten minutes ago. I don't know why you're trying to deny it, it's no big deal."

"It wasn't me."

"It was you all right. Either that or you've got a double. What's the matter man, you look as if someone just walked over your grave?"

"It's nothing. I'm all right."

But I was badly shaken. My colleague was naturally curious, but I fobbed him off and went into the courtroom. I found it difficult to concentrate on the trial and made several mistakes, on one occasion being reprimanded by the sheriff. I took whatever opportunities I could to look round towards the public benches, but saw no sign of the face that I was afraid to see. However, this proved nothing. As usual, the court was full of spectators seeking entertainment or a place out of the cold; during criminal proceedings, the public benches are a favourite haunt of interested fellow-criminals, the unemployed and other people with nothing better to do. I could easily have missed him in the crowd.

I believe in fact I did and that he must have seen and followed me. At any rate, a couple of days later, I had gone into the office early in the morning to clear up some deskwork before going to court. I had been working for about ten minutes when the door of my room opened suddenly and Valerie walked in. She had obviously thought the room to be empty – normally she would have knocked – and she looked considerably taken aback when she saw me.

"What's the matter?" I asked her.

She didn't immediately answer. Her astonishment, I fancied, was mixed with a trace of fear. "How did you get here?" she asked finally.

"The usual way. I came in early to get some work done."

"How long have you been here?"

"Am I under cross-examination?" I asked her lightly. "I've been here about ten minutes. Why?"

"But I've just seen you in the street!"

"What?"

"I saw you outside a moment ago. What's wrong, Mr. Middleton? What's going on? Are you all right?"

"Sit down, Valerie," I said. "Tell me what happened."

She took her usual place in front of my desk. She seemed a little reassured by the normality of my manner, but still looked uneasy. "I just saw you outside. Don't you remember? I don't understand how you could— "

"Where did you see me?"

"About a hundred yards from the office, standing at the corner. I was on my way in. It was only a few minutes ago. Don't you— "

"No. What happened?"

"You were about to walk past me until I said good morning. Then you stopped and smiled at me and said hello. I got the strangest feeling. It was as if — But this is ridiculous, Mr. Middleton. You must remember!"

"No I don't!" She looked frightened and I realised that I had shouted at her. I made an effort to keep calm. "I'm sorry Valerie. I'm not sure what's happening myself, but I'll try and explain in a moment. Just bear with me a little longer. You said when I spoke to you it was as if— ?"

"Oh I don't know, as if you didn't really know me but were pretending you did. And the way you smiled at me, it was really creepy. Then I asked if you were coming into the office, and you said that you weren't, not today, but that you would see me soon. Then you carried on, walking away from the office. I stood looking at you for ages until you disappeared round a corner. I didn't know what to think. Then I come into the office and you're here. I don't understand."

"I'm not sure I do either," I said. "It wasn't me, Valerie. If it had been, I couldn't possibly have got into the office before you. Did you notice anything else about this man? Was he dressed like me?"

"You were, I mean he was wearing a coat." Automatically, she looked over at the corner of the room, where my grey overcoat hung on a wooden hatstand. "It wasn't that one."

"Did you notice anything about his voice? Did he speak like me."

"No. Yes. I mean, it was like your voice, but— "

"Did he have a Glasgow accent?"

"Something like that. It was more as if, more—"

"More working class? Did he speak more roughly?"

"Yes, that's it. Mr. Middleton, I'm getting really confused."

"I don't blame you. So am I. It's like this, Valerie, there's a man going around who apparently looks like me. You remember that man Noakes I saw last week, the one who wouldn't let me act for him? He mistook me for this man. I don't know who he is, but he seems to be some kind of criminal."

"But that's awful! Shouldn't you tell the police?"

"What could I tell them? The man hasn't done anything wrong." The enormity of this statement stopped me short for a moment. "I mean," I continued, "I've got no real reason for complaint, no legal reason."

"But he looked just like you! I was sure it was you."

I got the impression that she was beginning to develop a supernatural fear, similar to my own. I didn't find this comforting. "Look," I said, "if you see him again, tell me immediately. And let me know if you hear of anyone else who's seen him."

"How will I know that it's him and not you?"

"I don't know. But I've a feeling that you'll be able to tell."

I don't think this enigmatic statement gave Valerie much reassurance. However, we dropped the subject for the time being and did our best to proceed with our work normally.

When I returned from court, just before lunch, I found that my request for further information had been granted much sooner than expected. I had arrived at the office that morning too early to have met any members of staff on the way in, and I was sure that I had not done so. Yet, according to Valerie, three other employees had seen me in similar circumstances to her own encounter. They had all spoken to me. Two of them I had ignored, the other I had reacted to in much the same way as with Valerie.

The two my double had not spoken to had been middle-aged women; the other was a young, attractive girl about the same age as Valerie.

I resisted the temptation to speak to the members of staff concerned, thinking it better to play the matter down. But that was not to prove easy. This haunting by my evil doppelganger continued over the next few days. Several other employees reported seeing me in the vicinity of the office, not only in the morning but at other times of day. At most of these times my presence could be accounted for somewhere else, in the office, at court or elsewhere. I confined myself to reports from Valerie, without directly confronting any of the people concerned, but, nevertheless, I felt an uneasy atmosphere develop around me at work. I was given sidelong glances, whispered conversations ceased at my approach and I was generally treated with a degree of reserve that had not existed before. None of this made me feel any better.

I felt the need to take some action, but was at a loss what to do. I had no grounds for going to the police unless I brought up the matter of the stranglings. But if I did that, the women at the sauna were liable to identify me as the killer, and I already knew that the real explanation was one the police would not believe.

The only thing I could think of was to confront him myself. This was something I both desired and dreaded. But how was I to achieve it? I had been keeping a lookout for my double; several times I thought I saw him, but lost him on pursuit. On another occasion, I thought I had caught up with him but found myself facing a stranger. I could not tell whether any of these sightings were real, or were all products of my over-stimulated imagination.

In any case, was it not normal for a spirit double to be seen by all except the victim himself?

I told Valerie to let it be known in the office that I wanted to speak to my double, and that anyone who met him should give him this message. The very next day Valerie herself saw him and passed on my request. However, he merely laughed and said that I would meet him soon enough.

After a few days, my double seemed to tire of his game and was not sighted again. However, by this time the story had reached my senior partner, Andrew Wintergreen, and he called me up to discuss it. With his usual excessive tact, he circled the subject endlessly; several times he looked as if he was coming in to land, but then took off again in another direction. Eventually, I gave him a little prompting. I was very busy and couldn't afford to spend the whole afternoon waiting for him to come to the point. Fortunately, I was well enough versed in his language to be able to cut some sort of path through the verbal jungle. "Is it about my double?" I asked.

He hesitated. He didn't like being asked such a direct, naked question, unsoftened by courteous preludes and digressions. It went against his deepest instincts and made him feel uneasy. "Ah — yes that was something I — I don't want to interfere, Ted, you know that, but, with respect, don't you think —? I mean, in the nicest possible way, isn't it —?"

"I've no idea who he is. I wish I did. I've tried to confront him myself, but he always seems to elude me."

"I'm sure you've done everything, everything possible, no criticism intended, none at all, but —"

"I can't go to the police. What could they charge him with?"

"Quite. Quite. I agree entirely." Andrew never actually disagreed with anyone; you knew he was unhappy if his assent was less enthusiastic than usual. "Just the same, there must be — I mean, some of the staff are getting quite — It's rather upsetting for them, bound to be unpleasant. Isn't there —? Who was that fellow who helped you with the Ogilvie divorce case, you remember the one who —?"

"Walker? I see, you think I should put a private investigator on his trail?"

"Ah — Yes!"

This was as blunt as he was ever likely to get. And he was right. It was the obvious solution. Walker, or any other competent private eye could quite easily keep a look out for my double and follow him. Giving him a description of his quarry would certainly pose no problem. Or he could pay Sammy Noakes a visit in prison and find out whom he had mistaken me for. One way or another, my double could be identified very quickly. Assuming, of course, that he wasn't a ghost.

I agreed to the plan. How could I do otherwise? Then, as I thought I was going to be able to make my escape, Andrew said, "Ted, is there anything about this — this business that you haven't—?

"No. What do you mean?"

"Oh nothing, nothing at all. It's just that, with the greatest respect, you haven't been quite your usual self recently. I've been worried about you."

"It would get to anyone, being haunted by their own ghost."

Andrew laughed. "Really, Ted. This fellow's as real as you or I, and we'll soon find out what he wants. But that's not what I mean. Remember, if there's anything I can — If there's anything you want to tell me — It won't go beyond this room."

I thanked him, but told him that there was nothing. What else could I say? If I had taken him up on his offer, some strain would have been put on his promise of confidentiality!

My partner's solution was of course the correct one. Walker was a good investigator who had done much work for our firm, and if my ghost was real he would soon find him. So why did I not immediately instruct him? Especially since I would not merely have been disposing of a nuisance, but taking a positive step to identify a mass murderer? Even now, when so much more has happened, I do not know the answer to this question. I know that I made no conscious decision not to hire Walker, but merely procrastinated, and my double's temporary withdrawal robbed the matter of any urgency.

In any case, I was soon overtaken by events.

THIRTEEN

TWO EVENTS of significance occurred in the week after my double's last appearance. The first was the discovery of Ann-Marie Colvin's body.

This by itself was not unexpected; it was more surprising that it had taken so long to turn up. Any lingering hope of her murder being imaginary had vanished during my last mental contact with the killer. *He* had remembered the Leith murder, and had consciously tried to improve upon it during his last venture; in his own evil way he was an artist, pursuing a forbidden path to perfection. And I could not doubt the reality of that last killing: daily articles in the press contrived to steer me firmly away from any such delusion.

It was never established what had kept the body submerged for so long. Perhaps it had lodged under some moored vessel, which had since been moved; perhaps her clothing had hooked on to some piece of sunken debris, eventually to be set free by the gradual pressure of the tides and the river current. At any rate, nearly six weeks after her death, she was washed up in Leith Harbour, giving a local dock worker an unpleasant start to his day.

Naturally the body was at first difficult to identify, but dragging of the river produced her handbag, and dental records provided the necessary confirmation. She had in fact been reported missing, but foul play had not automatically been assumed, as most adult disappearances are voluntary. Her father was dead and she had lived with her mother and stepfather, who had been absent on holiday at the time of her disappearance. She had not got on well with her stepfather. At work she had a history of absenteeism and had often spoken of taking off down south.

Ann-Marie Colvin sounded like a lonely and not very happy girl. Unfortunately, in trying to alleviate this, she had made a disastrous choice of company.

Although her identity was confirmed, it was less easy to establish the cause of death. But responsibility was provisionally allocated to the strangler, a reasonable and, as it happened, accurate assumption. However, this did not help the police much with their investigations: her first reported absence from work established the correct weekend of her death, but the exact time and place remained uncertain.

For me, the discovery was just another, incidental chapter in my unfolding tragedy. It did not materially affect my position, apart from throwing another log on to the flames of my self-recrimination. I thought of sending the police an anonymous letter, giving them the time and location of the murder. But if they traced the letter back to me, it was not difficult to guess whom they would arrest. And so I hesitated.*

---

*EDITOR'S FOOTNOTE: In fact, shortly after this time, the police received the following letter, whose author has never been traced. It was printed in letters cut from newspaper headlines, an unoriginal but effective way of concealing its origin:

ANN-MARIE COLVIN MET HER KILLER AT HAPPY JOES DISCO ON THE FRIDAY NIGHT 3 MARCH ABOUT 20 PAST 1. HE STRANGELED HER AND FLUNG HER IN THE RIVER LIKE A PEICE OF RUBISH, THEN THE BASTARD WENT BACK AND FINISHED HIS PINT.

At the time the police paid little attention to this, being one of many pieces of unsolicited correspondence. However, in view of the revelations in the killer's narrative, we are forced to regard the letter in an intriguing new light.

The second incident was more significant. For the first time I experienced mental contact with the killer without the added bonus of a new murder.

Once again he sneaked up on me in the night, with my defences down. As before, it was the intensity of his emotions that reached out to bridge the gap between our minds. But this time it was not the prospect of killing again that had aroused his passions.

It seems that killers have nightmares too.

Having said that, I am not sure if what was communicated to me was a dream or a waking recollection of a past experience. I am inclined to favour the latter. It had a horrifying coherence that was all too plausible.

FOURTEEN

I AM RETURNING from school through the grey streets of Glasgow's East End. Above, an overcast sky merges with the grime of the tall tenement buildings on either side. The people in the streets, shabby and bedraggled, match the surroundings perfectly. Already I have hung around the school area for as long as I could find companions. They stayed for a while, longer than they'd have done for anyone else, but now they have all run home to their mothers. All except me. I am dragging my heels, looking for detours, not wanting to go home.

I hate them!

For her I only have contempt, that woman who is not my mother. But him — Every part of my body is aflame with loathing for that man. He has given my life its meaning and purpose, if only I had the size and strength to carry it out. But soon he will be back in prison. He is never out for long. Stupid as well as evil. Not like me. They will never catch me. I am clever. And he knows it, in his own, drunken, moronic way he knows it. Taking it out on me, abusing me, beating me, while he still has the strength and thinks he has the wit. But I am cunning. In the end I will win.

Standing in front of the close, not wanting to go in. Right next door, the shuttered doors of the pub tell me that it's too early to go upstairs. While they're closed, he'll be home, begging money for opening time, looking for his small scapegoat to help fill the gap with a little brutality. Walking slowly up the dark close, which still smells of last night's vomit and piss. Avoiding the stairs, cutting through to the back court, the smell of the close now replaced by the stink of overflowing dustbins. Before me there opens a vast concrete expanse, where the back areas of the whole street come together. Other kids see me, call to me, invite me to join their games. Here I am appreciated, my worth is known, I am a natural leader. I despise them all, but they dance to my tune. Running around, kicking a ball about, climbing on the roof of the derelict air raid shelter, all the time exerting my natural power over my followers. "Henry, Henry, come up for your tea, Henry." Fuck her, she's seen me from the kitchen window. Ignore her. One of my companions mimics her, trying to mock me. "Your tea's ready Henry." But here, in my domain, I cannot be humiliated, such insolence cannot go unpunished. "Come here, Bruce McKee." Grabbing him, twisting his arm up his back until he sobs in pain. "What was that, you bastard? Say you're sorry. Go on, say it." "Stop it Henry, your hurting me, I'm sorry Henry." The others looking on, not daring to interfere. One last twist, to drive the lesson home, then he runs off crying and rubbing his arm. "Your tea's getting cold, Henry." What a fucking nuisance that woman is! Trying to make me look stupid in front of the others, another mummy's boy, just like them. But I showed them. "Henry!" Oh, to hell with it, I'm hungry anyway and these little bastards are boring me.

Thank God he's not at home, but her suffocating attention is almost as bad. "How are you dear, did you have a good day at school, what did they teach you?" Jesus Christ, I only went there to stop the truant officer from plaguing us. That fucking place is the biggest bore of all. This to myself, of course. I know how to keep her sweet, bending to my will. She thinks the sun shines from my little arse. If only she really knew what I thought of her.

Pie, chips and beans for tea. Again. No bloody imagination, that's her trouble. At least he's safely in the pub and I'm able to eat in peace. Pity it's in the same block as our house, or I'd set fire to the place. Maybe I'll do it anyway. What is there for me here? I might get rid of them both at once.

Later, back down in the cement playground, clutching the jam sandwich that is my special treat. "What did you get for your tea, Henry? I got fish and chips." "I got mince, what about you, Henry?" "Oh, nothing much. Minestrone soup for starters, then roast lamb with mint sauce. But it makes a change from the caviar." "What's that, Henry, what are you talking about?" Things I read in my mother's stupid magazine, you daft little cunt. "Oh, just some fancy grub you wouldn't know anything about." "I don't believe you, there's no such stuff as ca— ca—, whatever you call it." "You calling me a liar, Jim Robinson?" "No no, Henry, I was only kidding. Honest!"

I find a boy with cigarettes and bully them from him. Then, in behind the air raid shelter, me and my two closest followers, taking drags, coughing, slowly mastering a new adult art. More games, more assertion of my place as top dog. It gets dark. I move them to the far end of the block, out of earshot of our kitchen window.

"We should be going home Henry." "Damn you Sandy Thomson, you'll stay here if I tell you. You too Bruce McKee." "All right Henry." They play on in the dark, not daring to challenge me. But I am growing tired of *them*. I hide from them, sneak into a close, run home down the front street, leaving them to search for me in the dark as their parents grow frantic. I am laughing all the way. Stupid little bastards!

Up the close and dark stairs. Someone has smashed all the lights again and I have to feel my way. Ringing the bell, the door opening. "Where have you been, you wee cunt? Come in here." Oh Jesus Christ he's home early. Must have run out of money. Quickly, I try to back off, make for the stairs, but he grabs me and hauls me into the house, through to the kitchen. "I said where have you been, you little bastard?" What does he care where I've been, he only wants an excuse to beat me. Then I am over his knee, his strong tattooed arms holding me down, the smell of stale beer from his breath making me gag. My trousers are hauled down, the leather belt applied to my buttocks, again and again and again. Pain, growing worse, then numbness, not mattering any more. I clench my teeth, forcing myself not to cry, denying him the satisfaction. "Andy, Andy, leave the boy alone Andy!" Pleading for me, sobbing for me, but too afraid of him to interfere. Just like a bloody woman. Eventually he tires and stops. Later on he may beat her, if he can be bothered. But I don't care about that. Serves her right. Off to bed, in the bed recess in the big room, nursing my bottom until the numbness fades and the fire returns. Damn him, damn the bastard. I hate him. I'll kill him.

How many times have I said that now? A thousand? A million? He'll be back in prison soon, sure enough, like half the fathers in this block, but I can't wait. He deserves it now. He's deserved it for years. I don't need to be bigger than him, only smarter. And I'm that already. Still nursing the pain, my resolve strengthening.

What about my master plan? Would it really work?

Later on. The door opens, waking me. "Are you awake, Henry?" *I am now, you stupid bitch.* "Yes Mummy." "Did he hurt you, Henry?" *What the fuck do you think?* "I'm all right now." "I'll sleep with you tonight dear, make it better. He's no good for anyone in that state." *Jesus Christ, that's all I need!* "Thanks, Mummy."

She squeezes in beside me, her big flabby body pinning me against the wall. What sort of comfort is that? She tries to soothe me with her baby talk. I barely hold in my anger, hating her, hating *him.* Eventually she talks herself to sleep, leaving me awake, my nose pressed to the wallpaper. How I hate them!

I wait until I am sure she is sound. Nothing to be heard but her heavy breathing beside me and, faintly from the kitchen, his drunken snores. Now for it. I ease myself out from behind her, carefully, making sure I do nothing to wake her. Pause beside the bed. Good, she is sleeping on, undisturbed. Tiptoe out of the room, across the hall, into the kitchen, up to the bed recess, where he lies on his back, snoring, in the middle of the big double bed. Ideal. Now it's my turn, you big bastard.

Will I put on the light? No, can't risk waking him. My eyes are used to the gloom. Over to the sideboard, into the bottom drawer. Lift out the washing line, uncoil it. Back to the bed. Gently pull back the blankets, tying one end of the line to his wrist. Pause to check that he is still snoring. Good. I've thought it all out, so many times, it's got to work. Crawl underneath the bed with the rope, pushing it up between the bed and the wall. Back out, climb up on the bed, retrieve the rope end and pull in the slack. Coil it round his other wrist. Over the bed and under it again, softly and slowly, then back round, pinning him down on the mattress, not tightly enough to wake him, but leaving him no room for movement. Fasten the rope's other end to the leg of the bed.

He moves in his sleep and is hampered. Any moment he may wake. Move quickly, pull the pillow from beneath his head, place it on his face and sit on it, cutting off his air supply with my abused rump. He stirs, he struggles, but the ropes hold. I am not very big, but I am heavy enough. A grunting, a gurgling, but muffled by the pillow. Gradually growing fainter, dying out. His body wriggling, pulling against the ropes, then growing weaker. A final tremor. Then he is still. I stay where I am. Must be sure.

Wait a minute, what's happening? I feel movement. He is still struggling, has broken loose. No he hasn't. How can he? I know the end of this story. Yes there he is, not moving, the ropes still in place. But someone has broken free. A sound of coughing, followed by a woman's voice, high-pitched, terrified.

"Ted, what's got into you? Wake up, Ted!"

This has nothing to do with me. Never mind her, whoever she is. What about *him*, that bastard who has terrorised me for so long, who has beaten me for the last time? Is he dead? I sit on and on, my bottom on the pillow, the pillow on his face, just to be absolutely certain. For a long, long time there is no movement. I take off the pillow and look at his gaping eyes, the flecks of vomit on his drunken mouth. Yes, he is dead.

"For God's sake, Ted, you might have killed me!"

Who are you? Shut up!

Untie the rope, unwind it back round the bed. Roll it into

its coil again, replace it in the sideboard. Put the pillow back below his head.

Everything is now as it was before, except that the snoring has stopped.

"I've had enough, Ted. From now on I'm sleeping in the spare room."

Oh it's you, is it? Get out of my head! And take that fucking woman with you.

Back to the big room, where she still sleeps, undisturbed. Squeeze back in between her and the wall, my nose once more to the wallpaper. Must get some sleep before she rises and I am wakened by the scream from the kitchen.

Now all I need is to do something about her. Then I'll be an orphan again.

I hope they send me to a better place next time.*

---

*EDITOR'S FOOTNOTE: When Cunningham was ten years old, his stepfather died, having apparently choked on his own vomit while sleeping off a drinking bout. At the time his death was believed to be accidental. Is the above passage a wish-fulfilment fantasy, or did Cunningham's career as a murderer begin at a very early age? We will never know, but it is interesting to speculate.

FIFTEEN

FROM THIS TIME ON, my mental links with the killer grew more frequent. I found myself having further access to his memories and was able to find out more about him. In this way I learned further details about his childhood in the orphanage and series of foster homes, about his life of delinquency. It was a background that in every way contrasted with my own. Before long this information led me to a theory about him, which I decided to investigate.

But before I had done so, he had the notion for another murder.

I was alone in my office one weekday lunchtime, when the now familiar sensations began to intrude into my head. It was almost 1 p.m., I had just returned from a morning in court and was dictating letters into my tape machine in between eating a snack lunch. Most of the staff were out for lunch and I was virtually alone in the building. At first I only experienced a change of mood, without any accompanying sense impressions. I grew impatient with the bundle of mail before me and had an impulse to cast it aside. I felt an urge to do something more active instead. Its nature gradually took form in my mind. Soon I had identified it.

No, I said to myself. Not now. I'm much too busy.

I took note of this sentiment with a kind of detached horror. Was that the extent of my feelings about the matter? The interruption of my work? He was going to kill again, without even having the decency to let darkness fall. I had to do something to stop him. I reached this decision with a worrying lack of enthusiasm, but I reached it just the same.

I shut my eyes and attempted to project my mind towards his, trying to meet his as yet weak messages at some halfway point. The homicidal mood grew stronger, but there were still no visual or aural messages. I opened my eyes again.

Could I intercept him? Unfortunately, I didn't know where he was. At various times I had received images of different parts of Edinburgh, including the interiors of many pubs. Occasionally I had glimpsed inside his lodgings. But I had no idea where they were. So for the time being all I could do was try to strengthen our mental link.

Should I remain in the office? Could I risk being observed in the strange behaviour my union with the killer was likely to induce in me? I would greatly have preferred not to. But where else could I go? Jean was liable to be at home, and in any case it would take me time to get there. Anywhere else would be too public. At that moment the office would provide as much privacy as anywhere. It would be nearly an hour before most of the staff returned. I told the telephonist to stop all calls until further notice, then got up and locked the door of my room.

I sat back down behind my desk, shut my eyes again and covered them with my hands.

Right, you bastard. Where are you?

No reply. Only a growing feeling of anticipation, of elation. Mingled with a trace of — mockery?

You can't hide from me. Where are you, damn you?

My anger reached out towards him, matching my passion with his, strengthening the bond. Why was I so angry? Because he wanted to kill? Or because I was being left out of it?

At any rate it worked. Though my eyes were still covered, I began to see flashes of light, fragmented images, sounds that were alien to the office background. A splashing of water. Something gently stroking my face.

The image clarified and remained constant. I was looking into a mirror. At a face. My own face.

No, not quite. The hair was just a little too long, slightly more disordered. And the expression was one of confidence and self-satisfaction, emotions increasingly unknown to me in recent months.

He was shaving, grooming himself to appear attractive to a woman. Preparing to lure her to her death.

I'm talking to you, you bastard. Why don't you answer me?

Oh it's you again? My lawyer friend. What do you want?

The face in the mirror gave me a welcoming smile.

I want to know where you are.

Where do you think? I'm at home. What's it to you anyway?

You're going to kill again!

What if I am? Oh, I see. You'd like to come along. You fancy a second-hand thrill.

No!

Why are you getting so worked up? Have I hit the nail on the head? Or maybe you're looking for business. You want a murderer to defend. Well, they'll have to catch me first.

I want to stop you.

Do you really? Are you sure?

Yes, damn it! And I'm going to succeed.

We'll see about that. Like the police, you've got to find me first. Obviously you don't know where I am, despite all your prying. Well, let's not make it too easy for you.

You can try. But I'm on your tail and you can't shake me off.

He laughed. It was a sinister laugh, echoing from the tiled walls of that unidentified bathroom, winging across the city from the killer's mind to mine. To him my presence was a joke, a little bit of fun to add spice to his adventure. Well, we would see.

There was something about our exchange that at first seemed slightly out of place to me. It was the first verbal two-way link that we had formed, and something about it did not seem quite what I had expected. At the beginning I could not quite identify what was bothering me. Then it struck me. I had been expecting some mental equivalent of his rough, working-class accent. But what came across – was it his own words or my verbalisation of his thoughts? – was something much more suave. I caught a distinct flavour of his keen intelligence, free of the disguise which my middle-class preconceptions had constructed from his dialect.

This realisation was a timely one. Otherwise my class prejudice might have caused me to underestimate him.

He finished shaving, then took a shower. I felt the jets of water hit his skin, shivered with him at their first, cold impact, enjoyed the caress of the sponge on his body as the water grew warmer. Along with him, I felt invigorated as his purpose grew stronger and his anticipation heightened.

Also, although he said nothing further to me for the time being, I felt him taunt me, received his scornful challenge.

But, in doing so, he did me a favour. Unlike the previous occasions, it helped me to hold on to my separate identity. Instead of becoming caught up in his mood, my anger was fuelled by his attitude to me, filling me with a competing emotion, strengthening the two-way nature of our link, tightening the grip of my mind upon his.

I held on while he left the bathroom and crossed a carpeted hallway to a shabby room containing a bed, wardrobe and a bare minimum of furniture. I remained with him as he dressed in an open-necked shirt, jeans and black leather jacket, saw him smile sardonically at me from the wardrobe mirror as he combed his hair. I continued to cling on as he left the room again, out the front door, down a flight of stairs and into the street.

Now I would find out where he was!

But not immediately. We had just left a red sandstone tenement and were walking down a narrow street. A few hundred yards ahead I could see traffic lights and traffic cutting across our path, where our street obviously joined a main road. On our right was a row of nondescript, grey terrace houses. I could see no distinguishing landmark. We could have been in Edinburgh, Glasgow or just about anywhere in Britain. I wanted to look around me, help fix my bearings, but he was aware of my intention and kept his gaze firmly forward. He was playing with me, enjoying the additional element in his murderous game.

We passed a fish and chip shop, an old cinema now

converted into a bingo hall, another block of tenements with shops on the ground floor. The traffic lights drew nearer and the familiar maroon and white shape of an Edinburgh double decker bus passed along the main road. At least we were still in or near the city.

We reached the main road and turned into it. Surely here I would find a landmark? I saw a busy street with shops on either side and, in the distance, a church steeple. We were not in the city centre, but could have been just about anywhere else in Edinburgh. The killer continued deliberately to limit my field of vision by gazing firmly in front of him as if his neck were in a brace, only turning his head to avoid collisions with other pedestrians or getting knocked down at junctions.

Then, without warning, he went into a pub.

He obviously felt my frustration and a ghostly laugh penetrated my mind.

Still don't know where we are? Too bad.

Although I had more access to his mind than ever before, he could still keep things from me when his guard was up. But sooner or later he would let something slip. I nursed my rage and held on. I had more patience than him, more persistence.

We were in a small lounge bar. Like the street outside, it could have been located anywhere – alcoves with upholstered bench seats, low tables with burnished copper tops, furry red wallpaper, a jukebox playing at a bearable volume, the obligatory fruit machine. There were only two other customers, a middle-aged woman and an elderly man, sitting separately, each reading a newspaper. A sole barmaid held the fort behind the counter.

She was red-haired, pretty and aged about twenty-one. I felt his excitement grow. Without needing to play the fruit machine, it looked as if he might have hit the jackpot first time.

She seemed pleased to see him. After all, he was a good looking chap, and she looked as if she needed relief from the boredom. Ripe pickings indeed!

"Hullo," she said. "What would you like?"

"A pint of heavy." He sat down on a bar stool as she poured

the drink. "Quiet today, is it?"

"Deadly."

"It must get really boring."

"You're not kidding."

She gave him the drink and he paid for it. "Never mind," he said. "You've got someone to talk to now."

Smooth talker, aren't you?

Shut up, I'm concentrating.

But little concentration seemed necessary, I noted, as I continued for a time as a mute witness to their conversation. He enjoyed the same facility at getting to know women as I once had myself, and his technique was not rusted by years of happy marriage.

"What's your name?" he asked her eventually.

"Doreen. What's yours?"

"Ted."

You bastard! I felt a surge of panic, and his mocking laughter came back in response. What was he up to? Was he trying to implicate me in his crime? Did he know my surname? I wasn't sure.

But although he was reckless, he was not stupid. He knew that implicating me would also lead to him. He was simply playing with me again. She was happy to remain on first name terms only, so he ventured no further information.

I returned to my passive role as they continued to learn more about each other – or rather as he learned about her and fed her lies in return. She lived locally, with her parents, and was an only child. All this managed to come out without either of them mentioning where the locality was. However, I had been given something to work on. I could perhaps intervene psychologically, if not physically.

She seems like a nice girl.

No reply.

She deserves better, don't you think?

Still nothing.

An only child, too. It could finish her parents off, if any-thing happened to her.

A feeling of indifference fed back to me, along with a slight puzzlement. *So what? What's it to you?*

Can't you think of the consequences of your actions for once?

A dawning understanding, followed by a return of the mockery. *Oh, I get it now. You're trying to appeal to my better nature. Too bad pal, I don't have one.*

I believed him. The similarities I had noticed in our personalities had temporarily blinded me to the most basic difference of all: his complete lack of conscience, the absence of any shred whatsoever of human sympathy or understanding. There would have been as much point in appealing to the better nature of Satan himself.

I withdrew again for a while but remained absorbed in their conversation. At one point a banging noise intruded in the background, but I paid it no attention, remaining seduced by his seduction technique. Then, not long after, I heard the persistent ringing of a telephone.

The killer heard it too. "Aren't you going to answer it?" he asked the girl.

"Answer what?"

But the telephone was not in the bar, it was in my office, back in the city centre. I tried to ignore it, but it carried on ringing. I opened my eyes.

I was hit by double vision, as my room in the office imposed itself on the lounge bar scene. And, as our two-way link was now securely forged, the killer experienced it too.

"What's the matter?" asked the barmaid.

"Nothing. I'm all right." He groped towards his pint glass and took a quick drink.

"You looked as if you had a dizzy spell or something."

"I did, just for a moment. I'm OK now." *Answer that bloody phone, for Christ's sake! Tell them to fuck off.*

I located the receiver and put it to my ear. "Fu— ," I said, and managed to stop myself. "Hello?"

"Mr. Middleton?" It was Valerie.

"What is it?"

"What's going on? Why have you locked your door?"

"I'm busy." I forced myself to seem calm. It took a great amount of effort, but I just about managed it. It was vital that everything should seem as normal as possible. "Something's turned up that I have to work on. Could you see to it that I'm not interrupted?"

"What is it?"

"I'll tell you later. Make sure I don't get any more calls."

"Mr. Drysdale's coming to see you at three o'clock."

"Tell him to— I'm sorry, would you cancel it? This is much more important."

"But— "

"Please, Valerie, will you just do as I say? I'll explain later. I must go now."

She sounded unhappy but didn't argue further. I replaced the telephone receiver. Now back to business. For a moment, I looked around my room in alarm. Were its outlines becoming clearer, wiping out the anonymous lounge bar? I shut my eyes and concentrated on the fading image.

Still with us are you?

You can rely on it.

Good. Wouldn't like you to miss the fun.

My hatred swelled and the image grew strong again.

"Still with us?" asked the barmaid.

"You can rely on it."

"You're a funny one. Do you always have these absent-minded spells?"

"Don't worry. I can concentrate when I need to."

The barmaid's business remained slow and I received no further interruptions from my office. When the lounge bar closed at two-thirty, the barmaid and the killer had become alarmingly friendly. Without very much resistance, he had persuaded her to meet him outside.

"You'll need to wait till I've cleared up."

"How long will that take?"

"Oh, a quarter of an hour."

"Is your public bar still open?"

"Yes, but— "

"I'll see you there then."

"Well — we don't want them to know any more than they need to, do we?"

"Oh, I see. All right then, I'll see you in the *Crown* down the road. Will that do?"

"Yes, that's fine."

The killer's foolhardiness astounded me. He had been prepared to meet her in the public bar of her own pub, to display himself in front of other customers and the bar staff, and then take her off to kill her. He would have been as well placing a newspaper advert for witnesses. And all this within a few hundred yards of his lodgings! Only the girl's diffidence had forced him into more discretion.

My reaction must have fed back to him. *What's the matter with you now? Think I'm taking a chance?*

Well, aren't you?

So what? It adds to the fun. Anyway, it's my neck.

With any luck.

Oh, so it's like that?

The more chances you take, the sooner you'll get caught.

That's fine by me.

If you feel like that, why don't you report me to the police?

I already have.

This stopped him short. I felt a small glow of satisfaction. He might be well ahead in the psychological game we were playing, but at least I could still score some points.

So why am I still walking free? There was a delay, then I felt a new surge of his self-confidence. *Oh, I get it. They didn't believe you. They wouldn't, would they?*

Not then. But I've got more information now.

Oh have you? What's my name?

Henry Cunningham.

Very good. And where do I live? Where exactly am I just now?

During this exchange, he had left the lounge bar by its front entrance and walked the short distance along the main road to

118

his place of rendezvous. As before, he had continued to look firmly in front of him, giving me as few clues as possible. Once again I had received a glimpse of a fairly ordinary main street – shops, a couple of pubs, a building society, a bank – which could have been anywhere outwith the city centre. And yet I had a feeling that I had been there before, that the street was familiar to me. But I could not quite place it.

And now we were in another perfectly ordinary bar, with no distinctive features whatsoever. Even the name – the *Crown* – didn't afford much of a clue. In short, I was no further forward in identifying the location. And the killer was sipping a whisky, preparing himself for his next fatal conquest and recovering well from my attack on his confidence.

Doreen arrived and gave him a radiant smile of welcome that pierced my heart. In the face of such trust, such appalling vulnerability, how could anyone plan to harm her? I thought of the danger she was in and the flames of my rage were refuelled. In the past, when the victims had remained fairly anonymous casual encounters, I had been temporarily infected by the killer's homicidal lust. But while the murderer had discovered an additional kick in first getting to know his victim socially, this had exactly the opposite effect upon me. Over the short period during which I had eavesdropped upon his courtship of Doreen, I felt I too had got to know her, and I had grown to like her. And now I was determined to save her.

"Would you like a drink?" he asked her.

"Yes please. A gin and bitter lemon."

He bought the drink and they sat down together at a table.

Around them, the bar's inhabitants carried on the leisurely business of a midweek afternoon: the barman drying tumblers and watching racing on the TV, two men playing pool at an automatic table, several other men nursing slow pints through the long afternoon, all in all a scene where any sense of excitement was muted, any feeling of drama at its lowest ebb. And, in the middle of it, the Canongate Strangler sat drinking with his next intended victim.

SIXTEEN

"WOULD YOU LIKE ANOTHER DRINK?"

"I'd better not," said Doreen. "I'm on again tonight. Have one yourself, if you want."

"I'm not bothered. I'd rather have that coffee you promised me."

"Can't we go to your place?"

"It's miles away," said the killer. "I thought you said your parents were out?"

"Yes, but— "

"I only want a coffee."

"Oh, do you?"

"Honest."

She giggled. "What a pity. Oh, all right then."

I realised that it would soon be time to act. About my strategy, however, I remained unclear. They had still given me no clue about their whereabouts. When they emerged into the street, now arm in arm, I felt the same elusive familiarity about the area. But I still hadn't identified it when they turned off down a side street nor, a few minutes later, when they went in the front entrance of a modern block of flats.

I would have begun to despair, but I knew that he wasn't yet ready to kill her. Murder was still on the agenda, but not until later. He might still be able to hide the detail of his thoughts from me, but by now I was an expert on his moods. He was still far from the last gradient, the one leading up to that final, intoxicating peak. When he finally got there, I felt sure I would know. Meanwhile, I had also got an inkling of his immediate intentions, and I think they were very much as the girl herself suspected.

She took him into a top floor flat. It was well appointed and brightly decorated, though not quite in a taste that would have appealed to those in my New Town circles. They sat down together on a couch in the living room and it quickly became clear that drinking coffee was not a high priority for either of them.

I found myself in a moral dilemma, one that my middle-class upbringing didn't help me to resolve. I was already having to live with my self-disgust at the pleasure I had taken in his murder lust. Now he was about to make me into a sexual voyeur – the word is not even adequate to describe a vicarious experience in which all the senses are fully engaged. This should have seemed much less reprehensible than enjoying murder, but in some ways my distaste was just as strong. I felt I should try to withdraw from our mental contact for a while.

On the other hand, while I had no desire to kill Doreen, I too found her sexually attractive.

He sensed my difficulty and of course found it very amusing, even taking enough time off to taunt me.

Looking forward to some second-hand kicks, are you?

I didn't want to give him the satisfaction of a reply that was bound to be inadequate, but I had no need to say anything. I felt his soundless laugh yet again tease the corners of my mind.

Fortunately, Doreen was demanding all his concentration and he had no more time for me. I found that my attention was also fully captured as I accompanied them through to the bedroom. I don't know if I would have been capable, had I wanted to, of breaking the mental contact. But I didn't want to.

If I broke contact, of course, there was no guarantee that I would be able to regain it again. My respect for Doreen's privacy could well cost her her life. I believe I was right to stay on, though I am not sure if I did so for the right reason.

In recollecting my experience of the killer's lovemaking, I have tried to detect any element of emotional involvement with the object of his passion, any substance of real human feeling behind the expressions of tenderness which he so skilfully conveyed. But there was none. It was an act of animal lust, disguised by the finesse of a skilled actor. She was not going to melt his heart and make him repent of his real goal.

In the beginning, I had wondered if the killer was interested in sex, as he had never before interfered sexually with any of his victims. I now saw that he did have such an interest, and that the byways of the sick mind are indeed strange. He enjoyed murder, but he had no taste for rape. He would have had no compunction about the latter – he had no compunction about anything – but it so happened that rape did not provide the sort of thrill on which he was psychologically dependent. At one time seducing women had given him the necessary stimulus, and when that had palled he had moved on to murder. Now he was progressing yet further, to a combination of the two.

Nor, as I at first suspected, did his compulsion derive from any particular hatred of women. For all human beings other than himself, male or female, he entertained the same feelings of indifference and contempt. It was just that he got more of a kick from killing women. Perhaps there *was* a sexual element in his murders, one that involved an unconventional form of consummation.

"What's the time?" Doreen asked him eventually.

"Twenty five past four."

"We'd better get up. My mother'll be home at five."

Did that give him time to kill her and then get away? Yes, plenty of time. I was on guard, running through my contingency plans, ready to make my move. But I felt the killer lazily consider the possibility of immediate action, then shelve it. Killing her at home would be too easy, not enough of a challenge. And he was enjoying the game too much to let it end prematurely.

"So you want rid of me?" he said.

"No — you know what I mean."

"When do you have to be back in the pub?"

"Quarter to seven. Though I'll need to get my tea before then."

"There's loads of time. Why don't we go for a walk?"

"That's a good idea," she said. "Let's go down to the beach."

The beach! Now I had a proper clue. Were we back in Leith? No, there was no beach there. Portobello, that was it! The little seaside resort only a few miles from the city centre. The two pubs had been in Portobello town centre. I had been there often enough, but my brief glimpse through the killer's eyes had not revealed any of its more distinctive features. I now realised how cleverly he had kept me guessing. His lodgings could only have been a few yards from the sea, but he had carefully kept his back to it throughout his short journeys.

Now that I had some idea where they were, I had more than one choice of action. I could intervene psychologically, or I could try to get there physically. I could also phone the police, but could think of nothing to tell them that they were likely to act upon. If I tried to get to Portobello in time, how would I manage it, handicapped all the way by two sets of sense impressions? By taxi perhaps. If I found one quickly, I could be there in fifteen minutes. It might well scare the girl off to see a double of her companion homing manically in on them. She would be scared of the wrong man, but the result would be the same.

But there was one major flaw in this plan. The killer was now reading my thoughts as well as I could read his, and he would be prepared for me. I would have to give the taxi driver a definite place to set me down, and then bridge the final gap between us on foot. By then he would have had plenty of time to get her to a secluded place. I might well arrive only in time to be dumped with a body.

So it had to be the psychological approach. And for that I would need my full concentration, which would be best achieved if I stayed where I was.

I waited until they had dressed again and left the house. Then, as they made their way back to the town centre, I began my attack. I had already tried to appeal to his sense of compassion, and found it to be missing. I now decided to work on his instinct for self-preservation. I knew him to be impulsive and foolhardy, but not entirely stupid.

You're taking a considerable chance, you know.

Am I?

Of course you are. You live in this area, several people have seen you with her. If you kill her near here, they're bound to catch you.

So what? That's what you want, isn't it?

I don't want Doreen to get murdered.

Well, you're going to be disappointed. I'm going to kill her, and I'm not going to get caught.

Are you going to wait until dark?

I might do.

But she's due back at her work before then. You'll have to do it in daylight.

So I'll have to do it in daylight.

Doesn't that worry you?

Not in the least. Makes it all the more interesting.

I believed him. He was a compulsive liar, of course, but I could read his emotions and they confirmed what he said. He would risk everything for that additional thrill, that extra element of danger that had not been there before. So far, everything I had said was only confirming his resolve. I withdrew for a time to take stock, then tried a new tack.

I've telephoned the police.

No you haven't. I know what you've been doing. I know everything that you've been thinking.

I'm going to phone them now.

No you're not. You've already thought of that. You know they won't believe you.

I made another temporary retreat. He had no better nature to appeal to, he was insensitive to danger. Did he have any vulnerable area at all? They had now reached the main road and stopped at the junction. Across from them, a continuation of the road they were on led down to the sea, which could now be seen, a few hundred yards ahead, shining in the late afternoon sunlight. I could feel his plan taking substance, his anticipation rising. Once they reached the beach there would not be much time left.

"You've gone all quiet again," said Doreen.

"Have I?"

"Do you always have these absent-minded spells?"

"Sometimes. I told you before, I can concentrate when I need to."

She laughed. "I believe you now."

They saw a gap in the traffic and began to cross the road. I had another idea. I opened my eyes, superimposing a view of my office upon his vision. Then I looked towards the window, which was the brightest light source in my room. He stopped walking, confused and partially blinded.

"What's the matter?" asked Doreen.

A car horn blared and she quickly helped him across to the other pavement. I shut my eyes again until they arrived there safely. I didn't want to save her from the killer by getting her knocked down in the street.

"Are you all right?"

"Yes. Just a slight dizzy spell."

"Are you sure?"

"Yes, I'm OK now."

I opened my eyes again. *No, you're not.*

What the fuck are you doing?

What do you think?

Now I had got him rattled. I was making progress.

"You're not all right," said Doreen as they stopped again. "What is it?" She sounded worried and was obviously concerned about his health. That was ironic.

"I sometimes have trouble with my eyes," he said. "It's nothing serious. It'll soon pass."

No it won't. I left my desk and and went over to the window of my room, matching my daylight with his. My window looked west and the sun was visible, above the roofs of the city skyline. I looked at it as directly as I could, without hurting my eyes.

Will you stop that, you bastard?
Why should I?
You won't stop me killing her. I can do it by touch if need be.

I can spoil your enjoyment.
She'll still be dead.

"I think you should go home," said Doreen.

"I told you it'll bloody well pass!" She shrank back at the violence of his reply. He made an effort to control his surge of temper, realising that he could spoil everything by alienating her. "Let's go down to the beach. The sea air should help me. At least there's nothing I can walk into there."

She was mollified and they continued the short walk down to the sea. The street was quiet, with few other pedestrians to get in the way and, as he gradually got used to the double vision, he was able to walk normally. Doreen, in any case, was holding his arm and giving him guidance.

His confidence began to return. I had won a round, but he was fighting back.

I remembered a tactic I had tried on a past occasion. I left the window and switched on the room light, then sat down at my desk again and looked directly at the bulb. My eyes began to hurt and coloured spots danced before them, but I persisted. However, he was now used to my assaults and soon adjusted. I was casting a glare over his vision, giving him a viewpoint like an overexposed photograph, but he was still able to see well enough to get by.

Perhaps I could attack him on more than one front. I had already provoked his temper once, and he had found it difficult to control. With the visual problem already there as a constant irritant, maybe I could taunt him over the edge and he would scare her off. Unfortunately he knew what I was trying to do and was expecting it.

I suppose you think this sort of thing gives you some kind of status, makes you important.

No reply.

It's pathetic. You're pathetic. You're a piece of vermin, the lowest of the low. This girl is worth a thousand of you. What gives you the right to take her life?

I know what you're trying. It's not going to work.

I continued to ply him with insults and abuse, but though I got him more edgy and he flinched at the occasional jibe, I failed to push him over. Knowing what I was about and being determined to thwart me was his best defence.

I would have to change my plan again. And time was running out.

They had now crossed the promenade and were walking on the beach. Although my business often took me to Portobello, it was some years since I had been on the seafront. Despite my present preoccupation and the fact that I too was viewing it through a glare, I could not help being impressed afresh by the huge expanse of beautiful flat sand, about two miles long and, when the tide was out as now, more than a hundred yards broad. In summer it would be full of life, but in this midweek spring evening it was almost deserted – the shelters and rows of coloured benches strung along the promenade were unoccupied, the pubs and amusement arcades were closed, the wide foreshore flat and bare. About half a mile away, two people on horseback trotted along the beach, a little nearer a boy was exercising his dog on the sand and the occasional lone pedestrian walked along the front. Apart from that they were alone.

"Let's walk down to the sea," said the killer.

He was getting ready to make his move. He was going to murder her by daylight, in front of witnesses who were too far away to stop him in time. As he contemplated the grandeur of the gesture, the magnificent contempt it displayed for the rest of the world, my attacks were forgotten and his elation grew. He was now on that final gradient!

I found myself, as on previous occasions, being drawn into his mood, becoming caught up in his excitement. Without realising what I was doing, my eyes swivelled away from the light bulb, clearing his vision a little.

I realised what I was feeling, and recoiled from it in a

spasm of self-hatred. So violent was my emotional *volte face* that I felt it make a dent in his own mood. Not a significant one, but enough to be noticed.

Here was a new strategy. If I could be infected by his emotions, then he might be influenced by mine. He did not have a better nature, but perhaps that of another person could be temporarily forced upon him. I could not appeal to him by argument, but I might be able to stoke up the flames of my conscience and project it at him, providing some sort of counterbalance to his homicidal frenzy. I thought of the liking I had developed for Doreen, the feelings of tenderness her lovemaking had engendered, which he had simulated but I had genuinely felt. I thought of the long life she would be denied, of the husband and children she would never have. I did a tally of his murders so far, conjuring up the ghosts of the dead victims to accuse him: the crumpled body of Janet Brown, lying in the dark close off Lothian Road, the blood of Sarah Lawson staining the pavement in the Cowgate, the decomposed remains of Ann-Marie Colvin being fished from Leith Harbour, the pathetic, naked form of Vicki Walsh, lying on the massage table. A tidal wave of revulsion and guilt swept through me.

"Why are you looking at me like that?" asked Doreen.

"What? Oh, sorry. I was thinking of something else."

"It's really nice here. Nice and peaceful."

"Yes," he said, fighting back my attack and turning his charm back on. "There's no one to bother us. We could do anything we liked."

"Why? What were you thinking of doing?"

"You'd be surprised."

Doreen giggled. "What, here? In broad daylight?"

They were now walking beside the water. From this point, back across the broad foreshore, the promenade seemed immensely far off. A solitary cyclist passed along it, a small figure receding even further into the distance. The nearest human being was at least three hundred yards away. A few seagulls walked about the sand, scavenging, but they offered no consolation. Nothing could be heard but the lapping of the water and the occasional cry of a gull. Doreen and the killer walked hand in hand along the wet, corrugated sand, she enjoying a pleasant afternoon excursion with a new boyfriend, he rallying from my attack and preparing once more for his own move.

I stepped up the pace. I turned my mind to funerals, weeping relatives, floral wreaths and the solemn graveside oration of a minister. I showed him Doreen's parents, devastated by their loss, sinking into a premature decline. I visualised Doreen nursing a baby, saw the baby being snatched away. I imagined her vital, living, loving body lying still and cold. I projected towards him, at full volume, all the emotions that had previously been alien to him – guilt, grief, compassion, the burden of other people's pain. And yet more guilt.

"Why are we stopping?" asked Doreen.

"Give us a kiss."

She smiled. "Haven't you had enough?" But she willingly complied and inclined her face up towards his.

In a moment his hands were round her throat.

He had acted so quickly that even I was taken unawares. My surprise was nothing compared with hers, but even so, she rallied amazingly quickly and began to fight back. Was his grip a little less firm than usual, had my recriminating phantoms infused a little hesitancy into his resolve? I am not sure, but even if I had partially succeeded, it was not enough. In a few moments she would be dead. What else could I do?

I opened the top drawer of my desk, fumbled about inside it and brought out a cigarette lighter which I kept for the benefit of clients and other visitors who smoked. I struck a light and turned up the flame, creating a miniature flamethrower. Then I put my left hand over the flame and held it there.

He felt the sudden jab of pain in his own hand and his grip loosened. Doreen broke free, stumbled back and tried to run away. He grabbed her and pulled her back. I put my injured hand half inside the open desk drawer, braced myself and slammed the drawer shut.

We gave a unison cry of pain, and he let go of her again, holding his hand and nursing his apparent injury. Doreen ran off, staggering and coughing. He could easily have caught up with her, but the two horse riders had seen what was happening and begun to gallop towards the scene. Doreen started running to meet them. The killer hesitated for a moment, then ran across the beach, towards the promenade, past a solitary pedestrian, who stood staring at him, too frightened or too taken aback to intervene. One of the horsemen started off in pursuit, but the killer had a good start and soon lost his pursuer in the back alleys of the town.

His emotions still ran high, and his mood winged across the city rooftops towards me, like a black arrow. Curiously enough, he still felt no fear. But he still had murder in his heart, and now it was directed towards me.

I had succeeded. I had saved Doreen's life.

I noticed that my hand was hurting very badly.

SEVENTEEN

FOR A WHILE I sat on behind my desk, with no energy to do or think anything. My hand hurt abominably and looked a mess, with a bright red patch where I had burned it and a quickly developing swollen area around the knuckles. For some time, the killer's mind remained linked to mine; I'd had more than enough of him for the time being, but now found him difficult to get rid of. It was not because he wanted it that way – among other things, he was unhappy about continuing to share my self-inflicted pain – but the thoroughfare between our minds was now so well travelled that it was becoming difficult to block off.

I accompanied him by a devious route back to his lodgings, where he lay on his bed and continued to think murderous thoughts about me. There was a revolting childishness about his attitude, as if he were an immature delinquent who had been deprived of some deadly toy.

You bastard! Why did you have to do that?

You know why.

Why couldn't you mind your own fucking business? What's that little bitch to you? Now she'll go off and blab to the cops.

Good.

I'll get even, you wait and see. If they catch me, I'll say it was you.

I've got an alibi. I've been in my office all afternoon.

Bastard. A pause. *What did you do to your hand? It hurts like hell.*

131

It's all in your mind. Why don't you take an aspirin?

He continued to curse and berate me but, after a while, his mental signals grew weaker. Eventually, as if he were a little boy crying himself to sleep, he dozed off and the contact was broken.

I looked around my office, which once again had the only visual claim upon my attention. What next? I tried to analyse how I was feeling. I had saved a girl's life, literally snatched a victim out of the strangler's grip. I should have been feeling very pleased with myself. But instead I felt a curious sense of anti-climax, about which I felt a little uneasy.

I was saved from further depressing self-examination by a timid knock on the door of my room. I went over to the door, unlocked it and opened it. It was Valerie.

"Are you still busy, Mr. Middleton?"

"No Valerie, come in."

"The cleaners want to know if they can do your room."

"Yes. I'll be going in a minute. What time is it?"

"Ten to six. Everyone else has gone home. I waited on to see if there was anything you wanted."

"Thanks. Sit down for a moment and tell me what's been happening. Then you can go."

I sat back down at my desk and she took her place in front of me. "Mr. Drysdale wasn't very pleased. He says he's going to get another lawyer."

I sighed. "So we lose some. Anything else?"

"Mr. Robinson's coming back on Friday. And Mr. Wintergreen wants to see you. He says it's important."

I found this request from my senior partner a little ominous, but dismissed it for the time being. Valerie gave me a few other messages, but none of them was very urgent. "That's fine, Valerie," I said. "You can go home now. I'm sorry I kept you late."

She hesitated for a moment. "You've hurt your hand. What happened?"

I had been keeping my left hand out of sight, behind my desk, but now I had accidentally brought it back into view. "I got it jammed in my desk drawer. It's not as bad as it looks."

She must have been wondering how such an injury could have occurred by accident, but she didn't say anything more about it. However, she still seemed reluctant to leave. She appeared to be plucking up courage to say something, then, encouraged by my apparent return to normality, she let it out.

"I don't want to be cheeky, Mr. Middleton, but are you all right?"

"Yes. I told you, it looks worse than it is."

"I don't just mean your hand. I was worried about you. About this afternoon and everything."

"I had a bad time. But it's all right now."

"Did you get your — your work done?"

"Yes," I said. "I did a good afternoon's work. The best I've done for a long time." I saw from her reaction that this enigmatic statement was not going to help. "Anyway, things will be back to normal tomorrow. You go off home now."

She went away, without further persuasion. I could see that she was worried about me. Did her concern go beyond that of a secretary for her boss? I fancied that it did, just a little, and found the idea intriguing. Not for the first time, it occurred to me that here were easy pickings, should I ever decide to make a move. The strangler's recent conquests had reminded me of just how simple it was to get involved with women, if only I cared to get back in practice. And she really was a beautiful girl. In other circumstances —

I stopped these wayward thoughts short. I was a happily married man. Or at least I had been until recently, and hoped to be so again.

EIGHTEEN

ITELEPHONED JEAN to say that I would be late, then left
for home via the nearest hospital casualty unit. They dressed
and bandaged my hand, after X-raying it to make sure that
no bones were broken. I told them I had caught it in a door,
which was a little more believable than the drawer story. It
seemed to be an plausible explanation, so I used it for Jean as
well. She accepted it with very little comment. Our relations
were becoming increasingly formal these days.

Later on in the evening, while Jean was putting the
children to bed, I was sitting alone, half-heartedly watching
television, when I felt a curious mood come over me. It happened very gradually and I found it at first very difficult to
identify. It started when I began laughing inordinately at the
jokes on a mediocre TV comedy, then I grew morose and began
muttering to myself. For a while I did this half-consciously,
unaware of what I was saying; then some of the words began
to register. "Little bitch will blab to the cops," I was saying.
"Need to lie low for a while." And more in that vein.

Then I noticed that Jean was standing in the doorway,
listening to me. She wore an expression I was getting depressingly used to these days.

"Are you all right?"

"Yes, I'm fine." I found that I was slurring my words a
little.

"What on earth are you muttering about?"

"Nothing." I got up from my chair, staggering a little. "I

134

think I'll go to bed," I said, pronouncing my words carefully. "I've had a hard day and my hand's hurting. I'm dead beat."

She didn't argue and I made my way upstairs. As I entered the gloomy hallway and staircase, I fancied I saw patches of light imposing themselves on my vision. They began to take shape as I entered the spare room and lay down on the bed.

Jean and the children all now slept in the main bedroom, locking themselves in every night.

By this time my slow-working brain had realised that I was receiving another transmission from the killer. His intensifying emotions had once more bridged the gap between our minds. So strong was our bond becoming that something less than the prospect of murder was enough to open the passageway; in the present case, it was the mood brought on by his increasing drunkenness.

And, courtesy of his dwindling social security benefit, I was getting drunk along with him.

He was in a public bar, sitting on a bench seat with a whisky and a half pint of beer before him. He sat alone at his table, though otherwise the place was fairly full. It was an attractive bar, spartan in décor, but with large front windows, carved woodwork around the gantry and other simple features that gave it a distinctive character. This impression of my surroundings was obtained in brief snatches; most of the time his attention was concentrated on the table before him and on his own dark thoughts.

The bar seemed familiar to me, but I couldn't be sure. As I said before, I am not a habitual drinker – I think I have seen more pubs from inside the strangler's head than I have ever entered in person – but I had a notion that this one was somewhere in the city centre. It wouldn't be anywhere in Portobello, that was certain.

Drowning your sorrows, are you?

Fuck off, I've had enough of you.

The feeling's mutual, I can assure you. But I don't seem to have any choice in the matter.

Well, shut up then. I don't want to hear from you.

I haven't opened my mouth. Maybe I should have been a ventriloquist.

He made no reply, trying to ignore me. But his drunkenness, which I was sharing, was making me loquacious. And if I had found a way of annoying him, it seemed to me that he was fair game. It was definitely my turn.

So the police haven't caught up with you yet? Well I expect it's just a matter of time.

I wouldn't be so sure of that.

Why not? You can't afford to be seen much around Portobello.

I'm due to move out of there at the end of the week. I'm not quite as stupid as you think. I don't normally shit on my own doorstep.

I see. So you thought you'd give them a little parting gift, like a body on the beach. Too bad you didn't manage it. Still, Doreen will make a good witness, the best they've had so far.

Shut up!

Yes, she can certainly give the police a full description. I wouldn't be surprised if they were waiting for you when you got home tonight.

How could they be? They don't know who I am. There's no way they could be on to me.

I wouldn't bank on it. There must be a few people in Portobello who know you.

You're talking shit. I haven't stayed there very long.

Maybe, but it's a small town. You're probably quite a prominent citizen, a big handsome guy like you. Lots of people will have seen you around, including, I would imagine, some of the people in Doreen's pub. I doubt if it's the first time you've been seen in a Portobello pub. In fact, I'm sure Doreen herself could probably place you, if she puts her mind to it.

Why don't you fuck off, pal? I didn't ask you to come into my head. So you can get right back out again. You're beginning to get on my nerves.

Good. That suits me fine. The more you suffer, the happier I'll be. I didn't ask to get into your head either but we seem to be stuck with each other. In our case I agree that two heads are worse than one, but that's the way it seems to be.

Think you're very clever, don't you? Why don't you just leave me alone? Let me get pissed in peace. You've already buggered me up enough for one day.

Although this dialogue occurred entirely within our heads, his drunkenness had blurred the distinction between vocal and merely cerebral conversation. Like someone who cannot read without mouthing the words, his half of the exchange had begun to emerge in a form that was audible within the pub. Fortunately for him, it was unlikely that anyone would be able to make out the import of what he was saying. But he had drawn attention to himself as a drunk who was muttering to himself, a drunk, furthermore, who was not in a very sociable mood. My view of the pub was of course confined to the input through his blurred senses, but I gathered from the noises round about that people had begun to notice. One little extra push from me and something interesting might happen.

I'm glad I did something to bugger you up. It's about time somebody did.

I'm warning you!

About what? What can you do to me? Especially after you go back home to the seaside tonight and stagger right into the arms of the boys in blue.

"FOR FUCK'S SAKE PUT A SOCK IN IT!"

This was transmitted to me with some force; not only had it come direct from his mind to mine, but he had bawled it out aloud in the pub. Heads turned round, and everyone was staring at his corner. A barman left his post and came over.

"What's the matter, mate?"

"What? Oh, nothing. I'm all right."

"Are you looking for trouble?"

"No."

"Maybe you should go home. You look as if you've had more than enough."

"I'm OK."

The barman didn't look convinced, but left it at that. It was as well for his peace of mind that he was unaware of the murderous fury that was barely contained within his drunken customer. But I felt it. My strategy of baiting him was working well.

Getting touchy, aren't you?

Shut up!

I think if I work at it, we can get you flung out of here.

He retaliated by lifting his whisky glass and draining it in a single gulp. Then he did the same with his beer chaser and stood up. He staggered, clutched the table for support, and I felt a brief spasm of pain in my sore hand as his own hand temporarily took his weight. Out of the corner of his eye, I could see the bar staff watching him warily, but they didn't intervene, probably waiting to see what he would do first.

He went to the toilet. After he washed his hands on leaving – surprisingly fastidious behaviour from a drunk, especially one with his background – I found myself looking at his face in the mirror for the second time that day. It had changed considerably. In only a few hours it had acquired shadows. Gone was the expression of confidence and self-satisfaction. I saw a face that was haunted, the face of evil defeated.

And I was the good spirit responsible for the triumph.

He left the toilet and went straight out of the pub, his dulled wits functioning well enough to realise that he'd have more chance of getting served elsewhere. It was dark outside, but I could see that we were indeed in the city centre, in a side street near the University. It was the same locality as his second murder, the one which had given him his title. But at that time he had left no witnesses, so he was comparatively safe.

No witnesses, that is, apart from the unbelieved Edward Middleton, who was now taking his revenge.

I had been enjoying all this, of course, while lying on my bed at home. For once he was giving me a good dream rather than a nightmare. But there was no reason why I could not make it even better. While he was making his unsteady way towards the main street, I got out of bed and tried to walk to the bedroom door. As my lurching steps failed to synchronise with his, I seemed to have four legs, all trying to go in different directions. We both lost our balance and fell. I clutched the carpet, laughing wildly, as he hit the pavement and lay there.

When he tried to get back up, he put his weight for a moment on his left hand. I grasped my bandaged hand tightly and squeezed, treating us both to a sudden stab of pain. But I didn't mind, and laughed again as his hand gave way beneath him and he fell back down.

I managed to crawl to the bedroom door and pull myself upright. Then, just as he too had got back on his feet, drunkenly hauling himself up from the concrete slabs, I switched on the room light, blanking out his city street with a view of my bedroom. He cursed me and almost fell again as he walked into a lamp-post.

After a little more fun, I let him be, switching off the light and crawling back to my bed. I had thought of a more worthwhile strategy, a more pertinent way in which to haunt him. As he walked up the main street with as much equilibrium as his condition would allow, I renewed the moral attack I had tried on the beach that afternoon. One by one, I conjured up the dead faces of his victims, working myself into a righteous rage, projecting my emotion towards him, a scalding beam of recrimination. The second-hand effect of his drink upon me made it easy to whip myself into sufficient fury; the catalogue of his abominations was indeed a nauseating prospect for any normal person. As I paraded the corpses before him, I flung my feelings at him with all the mental force at my command. He staggered under the onslaught and clutched his head.

"STOP THAT, FOR CHRIST'S SAKE!"

Through his eyes, I saw the bottom half of a pedestrian, giving this apparent maniac a wide berth. I had drawn blood, but perhaps not in the most effective location. I decided to give him a temporary respite.

I let him carry on up the street and into the nearest pub, where he ordered a whisky and a beer. The barman looked at him suspiciously, but business appeared to be bad, so he decided in favour of taking the money. Then, after his first sip of whisky, I renewed my attack, with increased force. My first rage had not entirely subsided – it was sincere enough after all – and before long I managed to rouse it again.

I had now worked out my campaign plan. On the beach that afternoon, and again a few minutes before, I had given him a review of the corpses, a checklist of his victims as he last remembered them. That had had some effect, but it was not enough. For him to properly appreciate the consequences of his evil acts, it was necessary to fill in some background details of the lives he had wantonly cut short. Having closely followed his case in the media, I was well equipped to present a few of the facts to which he had been so callously indifferent.

Victim No. 1: Janet Brown. Aged 21, student at Edinburgh University. In the final year of an honours degree in English and History. Intending to become a school teacher like her mother. Father a doctor. Two brothers, one older and one younger. Attractive girl, intelligent, and well liked by her family, friends and all who knew her. Regular boyfriend, with whom she had fallen out a few days before her death. Little doubt that, given the chance, they would have made it up again. 1st mistake: to go to a disco without him. 2nd mistake: to walk alone the short distance from the Grassmarket to Lothian Road. Was either of these a capital offence?

What the fuck's this all about?
Hang on. You might learn something useful.

Victim No. 2: Sarah Lawson. Shop assistant, aged 22. Only child of an elderly couple. Quiet girl, not particularly beautiful, but with an attractive personality. Had been going out with the same boy since school and had been due to marry him in a few weeks time. Her parents had taken her death very badly, and her father had since suffered from a stroke, probably brought on by his grief. Her crime? To feel safe a hundred yards from her home.

This is becoming a real drag.
Don't take it like that. I'm trying to teach you something really worthwhile.
What's that?
How to be a human being.

Victim No. 3: Ann-Marie Colvin. Bakery worker, aged 20. Something of a loner, not very popular with her fellow workers. Devoted to her father, who died when she was 13. When she was 15 her mother had married again. Did not get on well with her stepfather who, if a certain Sunday newspaper is to be believed, made sexual advances to her. Thinking of leaving home. Was experiencing an unhappy period in her life which might have passed, given the opportunity. Her offence? Loneliness.

Did her old man really come on to her?
So it said in the paper.
That's really sick. Trying to screw your own daughter.
Stepdaughter.
Almost as bad.
But not a fate worse than death. Death is still the worst of all. The bastard who killed her, he's the one that should really be strung up.
Get to fuck!
Temper!
Anyway, don't give us any sob stories about that next bitch. She was nothing but a common whore.
You'd be surprised.

Victim No. 4: Victoria Walsh. Prostitute, aged 23. Middle-class girl from a good home. Married an out of work musician who had got her pregnant. Abandoned by her husband and left to bring up a young son on her own. Working in a massage parlour while studying for an Open University degree. Crimes: 1) Trusting the wrong man. 2) Earning her living by giving men pleasure. 3) Trusting the wrong man for a second time.

Is that right? That she had a kid?
So they say. Don't you read the papers?
What happened to him?
Who knows? They probably put him in an orphanage.

This silenced him for the time being. Had I made an impact on him, found a crack in the armour plating that surrounded his heart? I had certainly made an impression on myself. My rage at his crimes was beginning to boil over. I stepped up my attack, abandoning the life histories and returning to the corpses. I gave him the full gamut of dead bodies, weeping relatives, funerals, outraged articles in the press. As my anger mounted, as I felt prepared to strangle him myself had he been within reach, I accompanied the accusing visions with a verbal commentary. *This is your work, you vermin, you fiend, you beast, you monster, you filth, you excrement, how dare you, what right do you have, look at them, look at all of them, these girls, these innocent girls, all dead, every one, all these lovely girls, all these lovely lives, brought to an end, just because of you, it was you, look on your work and tremble, what kind of person are you, don't you know what you've done, well there it is, you did it, it's your fault, it's all down to you, the buck stops with you, you're the one, you're responsible, it was you you you you you you you you you, you're guilty guilty guilty guilty guilty guilty guilty guilty guilty—*

His resistance didn't last long. *"FUCKING STOP IT YOU BASTARD, STOP IT, STOP IT, STOP IT, STOP IT— "*

The barman didn't need any further excuse. "Right pal, time to leave." The murderer looked at him blankly, through punch-drunk eyes. "Out," said the barman, and took his drinks away.

This action finally registered. He tried to get his drink back and collapsed over the counter. "Gi' me my fuckin' dring back, ya cun'."

In a moment the barman was round the counter and frog-marching him out. He was flung forcibly out of the door and fell across the pavement, face to the kerb.

I too felt the impact of his body on the cold stone, the crack of his head on the hard surface. But I didn't care. I enjoyed it. *Now you're where you belong, you swine. In the gutter.*

It was nice being involved in all this drama while lying safely at home in bed. Before long I drifted into sleep, feeling happier than I'd been for months.

NINETEEN

ONE GOOD THING about vicarious drunkenness is that it doesn't leave a hangover. I was therefore in reasonable shape next morning to start picking up the pieces of my professional life. My morale was given a further boost when I saw that the results of my unknown act of heroism dominated the front pages of all the papers, national and local. One particularly lurid piece sticks in my memory:*

FIEND FOILED IN DAYLIGHT DEATH BID
LOCAL HEROES GALLOP TO RESCUE

A Portobello barmaid narrowly cheated death yesterday afternoon at the infamous hands of Edinburgh's Canongate Strangler. And the notorious monster, wanted for the callous slaughter of four young women, had the sheer nerve to make his attempt in broad daylight and in front of witnesses!

Attractive local barmaid Doreen McArthur (20) made her miraculous escape on the broad and beautiful sands of Portobello beach, managing to break free after the fiend's fingers were actually round her throat.

Kiss of Death

"It was horrible," said brave beauty Doreen. "He seemed so nice. He was in the pub at lunchtime and we got talking. We went for a drink after I finished work and then had a walk on the beach. He asked to kiss me and then, before I knew what was happening, he suddenly began to strangle me. I don't know how I managed to get free."

---

* EDITOR'S FOOTNOTE: The article to which the narrator seems to be referring is here reproduced in full for the reader's edification.

The murder bid was witnessed by horse riders Andrew Paxton (25) and Patricia Robertson (23) who were further along the beach when they saw the strangler strike. While Patricia went to the aid of Doreen, Andrew galloped after the killer, but he shook off his pursuer in the back streets of the attractive resort.

Eye Trouble

Doreen describes her attacker as being in his late twenties, about six feet tall, with dark hair and an attractive appearance and manner. He wore a black leather jacket, blue jeans, a white shirt with an open neck and spoke with a Glasgow accent. He gave his first name as Ted, though this is thought to be an alias. But the most interesting revelation is that the killer may have trouble with his eyes – several times he became afflicted with what he called a "dizzy spell", and later "eye trouble", and seemed to be partially blinded for a short period of time. This may prove to be the most significant clue so far in tracking down the maniac who has terrorised Edinburgh since the beginning of the year. Chief Superintendant James Montgomery, the police officer in charge of the strangler investigation, said last night, "We now have our best description so far of the killer. He cannot escape justice for much longer."*

I was helped to catch up with my work by being left largely free of further mental intrusion from the strangler. Occasional flashes told me that he had confined himself to his room for the time being, a sensible precaution in the circumstances. I was

---

*EDITOR'S FOOTNOTE: It will be noted that at this stage Doreen McArthur did not admit to any intimacy having taken place between her and her attacker. However, she later confessed to it in a Sunday newspaper article entitled *My Afternoon of Passion with the Strangler*, no doubt after a substantial payment of money had helped overcome her modesty. By this delay, she robbed the police of the opportunity to check her home for fingerprints, which might have considerably shortened the investigation, as Cunningham had a criminal record and his prints were already on file. Unfortunately, the most recent police photograph of him was twelve years old and showed him with a beard and much longer hair. Also, this part of the narrative seems to suggest that the story of the eye complaint might have been a red herring. Certainly, no trace of it was detected in medical examinations made of Cunningham in prison. The resulting confusion was not helped by certain press articles (*Myopic Murderer, Strangling Can Make You Blind* etc.).

also spared having to share the hangover from which he was undoubtedly suffering. By lunchtime I was well on the way to making up my backlog, and Valerie was looking more and more relaxed in the face of my apparent normality.

My senior partner, Andrew Wintergreen, was engaged all morning, but we managed to catch each other free just after lunch. He had not said what he wanted to see me about, but I had a suspicion, which proved to be correct. By his standards, he got to the point fairly quickly, though it still took him some time. Usually I could shorten our conversations a little by some tactful prompting, but this time I left him to it. If his message had got lost entirely, I would have been quite happy.

He had, of course, an easy talking point to start with. "What happened to your hand?"

"A silly accident. It got caught in my desk drawer." It sounded very feeble, but I thought it preferable not to change my story from the one I had told Valerie. Better one unconvincing explanation than two conflicting ones.

"How on earth did you manage that?"

"I'm not quite sure. I was searching through my desk in quite a hurry."

"I see," he said. He didn't sound convinced, but he was far too tactful to say so. "Nothing broken, I hope?"

"No, I had it X-rayed at the hospital. It should be OK in a day or two."

"Good, good. I'm glad to hear it." He looked at me thoughtfully for a while. He seemed unhappy and considerably embarrassed. Once again he had been silenced by the want of a sufficiently diplomatic opening. Then he sprang into decisive action and opened his desk drawer.

He brought out his cigarette box. "Cigarette?"

"No thanks, I don't smoke."

"No, of course not. But don't I remember —? No, I must be mistaken." He replaced the box in his desk. He looked at me appealingly, hoping I would help him by raising the subject myself. But I left him to it.

Eventually he said, "Ted— "

"Yes?"

"I wanted to— I wondered— Ah— are you happy with the new waiting room?"

"Yes, it's fine."

"Yes, yes, I thought so too. It's much better now, much better."

"Yes, it does its job. It segregates the scruff who come to see me from the respectable clients."

"That's not what— I didn't— "

That was exactly what he had intended, but he didn't like hearing it stated so baldly. I found I was getting unusually irritated by this interview. I was in a mood, not just to be unco-operative, but to be downright obstructive. But I didn't have much longer to wait. Seeing that he was going to get little support from me, he finally plunged straight in.

"Ted— "

"Yes?"

"Yesterday afternoon."

"Yes?"

"What was— I gather you—"

"I was rather busy. I asked not to be disturbed."

"Yes, so I gather. What was it that was so urgent?"

I had known that he would eventually get to this question and was prepared for it. "I was behind in my work for the McQueen trial tomorrow. I spent all of yesterday afternoon and evening on it." This was a fairly safe story. My partner knew that it was a big trial and required a lot of preparation, but he didn't know that I had already spent most of the previous weekend working on it. No-one else knew that, not even Valerie. Although he had some tiresome qualities, I liked and respected Andrew Wintergreen and would have preferred to have been honest with him. But what other explanation could I give? That I had been in mental communion with the Canongate Strangler and had managed to save his latest victim? I don't think that would have helped.

As it was, enough damage had been done. Now that he was firmly on course, he managed to stick to it with remarkably few deviations. "Was it so important that you had to cancel Ken Drysdale's appointment? He phoned me up later and complained."

"Yes, I'm sorry about that. I think I might have panicked a little."

"That's not like you, Ted. Not like you at all. Also— " He paused again, looking even more embarrassed. "Some of the girls were saying that they heard some— some strange noises coming from your room."

"I think I cried out when I hurt my hand."

"I believe they said it was more than— Anyway, Ted, you're not under cross-examination. I just wanted to— I've been a little worried about you lately. I think you've been working too hard, feeling the strain a bit."

"You may be right. My wife thinks I should see a doctor."

"That sounds like a good idea. And try and fit a holiday in soon. I think you need a break."

"I'll do that."

Even though I knew it would do no good, I had already decided to visit my doctor, if only to convince Jean that I was trying to do something about the problem.

"There's one more thing," said Andrew. "What happened about that fellow who looked like— The one who was bothering the staff?"

"He hasn't been seen again. Not since the last time we discussed it."

"Did you have him— did you put someone on his trail?"

"I never got round to it. After he disappeared, there didn't seem much point."

"Just the same, it might have been a good idea. If only to— Anyway, I take it that yesterday had nothing to do with— that he hasn't been bothering you again?"

"No."

This was an outrageous lie, but as our meeting wound down with some bland small talk to cushion his unaccustomed mood of frankness and plain speaking, I did not think that I had been entirely dishonest. I really felt that I was beginning to get my problems under control. The strangler was not pestering me any more. For the moment at least, I had the upper hand.

This new mood of self-confidence suffered a slight setback later that afternoon when Valerie brought me a bundle of mail to sign.

She seemed a little hesitant. "It's one of the letters on your last tape," she said.

"What about it?"

"I was a bit puzzled. I've typed out exactly what you said, but I thought I'd better speak to you about it."

I took the letter from her and looked at it. It was a letter to an insurance company, denying our client's liability in a motor accident claim. Typed neatly by Valerie on the dignified notepaper of Summers & Wintergreen, the contents appeared all the more incongruous:

> Dear Sirs,
> Don't give us this shit, it wasn't our man's fault, so why don't you tell your man to get to fuck and get off our back? If you don't, I might be paying you a wee visit.
> Yours faithfully,
> The Canongate Strangler.

As Valerie stood before me, waiting for an explanation, I felt my face go red. "It was— I meant it as a joke," I said. "I thought I'd scrubbed it."

"Oh, I see."

"Not in very good taste, I agree. I'm sorry. Have you still got the tape?"

She gave me the cassette and, after she'd gone, I found the letter and played it back. It was dictated in a rough Glasgow accent, and was barely recognisable as my voice. I had no recollection at all of having dictated the letter.

It looked as if the killer was beginning to fight back.

Maybe it *was* time I had a holiday.

TWENTY

ON THE FOLLOWING SUNDAY my mother came to dinner. We usually saw each other about once or twice a month, though Jean visited her with the children a little more often. Since my father's death, my mother has lived alone, in the Morningside area of the city. My father left her comfortably off, though she moved to a smaller house for ease of maintenance. She was now approaching seventy, but still kept in good health.

I suspected that Jean might have confided in her about my recent behaviour, but so far my mother had not raised the subject with me.

I had decided that it was now time for me to speak to her about it. I was ready to test my theory about the murderer. I had almost raised the subject with her several times before, but had put it off, reluctant to hear the answer. Now the attempted murder of Doreen McArthur had brought matters to a head.

After dinner, I asked my mother if I could speak to her alone. Jean made no comment, and even looked a little relieved. We went through to the sitting room at the back of the house. Jean served us tea and then left.

My mother herself didn't seem particulary surprised by my request. Obviously Jean *had* told her of our troubles, and she was now expecting me to take her into my confidence.

"Jean's been very worried about you, Ted," she said.

"I know. Things have been difficult lately."

"Is that why you want to talk to me? I don't want to

interfere between you, but if there's any way I can help— "

"It's not a marital problem, at least not in the usual sense. It's not Jean's fault at all, and there's no-one more sorry than me at the way she's been affected."

"She's been trying to get you to see your doctor."

"I know, I've agreed to it. I'm going on Monday. Though I don't think it'll do any good."

There was a pause as I tried to think of the best way to broach the topic. I was not finding it easy. All my adult life, I have had a strong instinct to regard my mother as someone who needed to be protected from the harsher realities of life. She has an air of vulnerability, which has nothing to do with her advancing years; I think it is something she has always possessed, a legacy of her upbringing in the more sheltered backwaters of middle-class Edinburgh. I knew this appearance to be misleading and that she possessed much strength of character, unobtrusive qualities of endurance, tenacity and other introverted virtues not obvious on the surface; that even a little of her character eventually managed to rub off on me is something for which I have become increasingly grateful. And yet she still seemed like a gentle lady, with whom one does not like to talk about certain things.

As I tried to work out what to say, I brought out a cigarette and lit it. I drew the smoke deeply into my lungs as I searched my mind for ideas.

My mother looked at me in some surprise. "When did you start smoking?"

"What? Oh, just recently."

"But you've never smoked in your life before. You were always against it. You saw what it did to your father's health."

"I know. It's just the occasional one. As you've gathered, I've been under a bit of a strain. It helps a little. I'm sure I'll give it up before long."

"I hope so. Anyway, are you going to tell me what this trouble of yours is all about? I'm surprised you haven't been able to confide in Jean. I thought you two were very close."

"We are, that is we were. But it's not easy. To tell you the truth, Mother, I'm not sure I can even tell you. Not everything. But there is a way that you might be able to help me, and that's why I wanted to talk to you."

I could see that what I had said so far was only adding to her confusion and worry. I decided that I would have to tell her *something*, or at least find some way of setting her mind at rest. But first the information I needed. "It concerns my background," I said.

"Your background?"

"Yes. I was adopted, wasn't I?"

I don't think my mother had known quite what to expect, but it was not this. "You know you were," she said. "We never kept it a secret. We told you as soon as we thought you were old enough. I don't understand, Ted. What's this all about?"

"Bear with me," I said. "I knew I was adopted, but I never learned much more than that. Do you know anything about my real parents?"

"A little. Not very much."

"Did they have any other children?"

"I still don't understand. Why do you want to know this?"

This was the moment. I still hesitated, but there was no going back now. "To be more specific, did I have an identical twin brother?"

My mother did not immediately reply, but her reaction told me the answer. I have never seen anyone so astonished. "How— " she managed eventually, "How could you possibly know that?"

"So it's true?"

"Yes. But how did you find out? Have you met him?"

"No. That is, not exactly." I could see that I was heading for difficulties. "I haven't actually met him, but I've heard from him. He's living in Edinburgh."

"So are you going to meet him?"

"I think it's inevitable."

"And is he the cause of your problems?"

"You could say that."

"But why?"

"It's difficult to explain. You see, Mother, he didn't quite land as lucky as I did. His background was, to say the least, underprivileged. I don't think it exactly helped his development. You remember you used to have a bit of trouble with me as a boy?"

"I'm not in much danger of forgetting. You were continually in hot water at school, always up to some kind of mischief. You nearly drove your father and I mad at times."

"Weren't the police involved once?"

"Yes, but your father managed to get it sorted out. It was a minor incident, a long time ago. You were never a *bad* child, Ted – wild, impulsive, thoughtless, maybe. Difficult to discipline. But never nasty, never mean. And you grew out of these problems years ago. All this is history. I'm sorry, Ted, but you've entirely lost me. I don't see why this is something that needs to be dragged up."

"Unfortunately," I said, "I'm afraid that it does. You see, I think my brother had something of the same tendencies. And he hasn't managed to outgrow them. He seems to have turned into some kind of criminal."

"I see. And has he been bothering you?"

I told her of my meeting with the criminal Noakes, who had been so terrified of me, and of my double's haunting of the office staff. These items, at least, were not secrets.

"And you've heard from him since?"

"Yes."

For some time, my mother had been growing more and more upset. Now she broke down and began to cry. I did my best to comfort her, feeling like an oaf who had knocked over a piece of Dresden china. I had tried to be as tactful as possible, but the material didn't make it easy.

Of one thing I was now certain: the full horror of my brother's atrocities must be kept from her at all costs.

After a while she calmed down a little. When I thought she had sufficiently recovered, I said, as gently as I could, "Why did you never tell me about him, Mother?"

"Would it have helped matters? Would it have stopped him

153

doing— doing whatever he's done to you?"

I sighed. "No, I don't suppose so. Not in the long run."

"You see," she said, "we thought it might upset you if you found out. We knew how close twins could be. When your father and I adopted you, we had the opportunity of taking him as well, but we weren't sure if we could cope. We were both getting on in years and one child seemed a big enough responsibility. We often wondered what had happened to him, if we had done the right thing in separating you."

"Of course you did. You saw what a handful I was. Could you have coped with two like that?"

"I don't know. But now you tell me these things about him. I can't help feeling guilty, somehow responsible."

"Look Mother," I said. "You acted for the best. You didn't make him into a criminal by not adopting him. But maybe you stopped me from becoming one. You always gave me the love and security I needed, but you disciplined me as well. You taught me how to curb my impulses, how to tell the difference between right and wrong. It was a hard lesson but I learned it. You had a difficult course to steer, but you got it exactly right."

A touching speech! Why don't you give it a rest, for Christ's sake? You're making me want to puke.

Who invited you?

I wouldn't miss a family reunion, now would I? Even if I am the black sheep.

You're no member of my family!

I thought you'd just decided that I was – brother! It certainly took you long enough to work out the obvious. How anyone so thick could get to be a lawyer beats me.

It occurred to me before. I just didn't want to admit it.

Not good enough for you, am I? Well that's too bad. You're stuck with me. We're two of a kind.

A genetic accident, that's all. That's where the connection ends. Apart from that, I'm no more like you than— than—

A face in the mirror? I wouldn't be so sure of it.

"What's the matter, Ted?" asked my mother.

"Sorry?"

"You look so strange — so grim. Are you all right?"

I realised that the emotions invoked by my silent dialogue must have been trooping across my features like some grotesque piece of mime. I began to appreciate just how peculiar my behaviour must have been appearing to those close to me. I made an effort to ignore the mocking voice in my head. I had put my mother through enough for one evening. "I'm sorry, Mother. I'm all right. Let's rejoin Jean and the children."

"But you haven't really told me anything about your problems. Apart from the fact that it's got something to do with your brother."

"There's not a lot more I can tell. But what you've told me is a big help. I think I can get things sorted out."

She still wasn't happy, but we left it there.

The nature of her revelation continued to fill my thoughts, long after my mother had gone home, long after the children were in bed and Jean had followed them. I was a blood relation of the strangler; more than that, I was genetically identical to him. If any of his vicious tendencies were inherited, they were somewhere in me as well. I shouldn't have been surprised by the confirmation of my theory. My relationship to the killer was the most rational explanation so far of my recent fantastic experiences: if telepathic communication is possible – and I now know it to be so – it must occur more easily between two brains that were cast from the same mould. Even so, I think it is understandable that my blood tie to such a monster was something I had been reluctant to face.

How had we managed to turn out so radically different? Did the same evil lurk somewhere within me, buried under the deep encrustations of middle-class respectability, a black diamond that the killer's mental digging was slowly bringing into view? Yet, according to my mother, my youthful wildness was never of an evil nature. Was his real viciousness something acquired later, from a life of continuing deprivation? Or was the first seed sown right at the beginning, when he was abandoned in the orphanage, without a proper parent figure to relate to?

Give it a rest, for God's sake! You're beginning to sound like a fucking social worker. I've had my fill of them.

It didn't seem to do you any good.

Just as well. Otherwise I might have turned out like you, a stuck-up, self-righteous prick. But you've got nothing to feel smug about. Your first idea was the right one. Underneath it all you're no better than me. We're exactly the same, only they stuck a silver spoon in your mouth. I had to fight for survival.

So killing women's a survival tactic?

No, it's just one of life's little pleasures. And one you quite like yourself. Come on now, admit it.

No!

Doesn't it turn you on, just a little?

You're revolting.

If that's the way you feel, why don't you report me to the police?

I told you before, I already have.

But you know who I am now. You could convince them if you really tried. What's stopping you?

Nothing at all. In fact, you're doing a good job of talking me into it.

That finally shut him up. But it was a long time before I got any sleep. The evening had given me much food for thought.

TWENTY-ONE

WHY DID I NOT report the killer to the police?
I am still unsure of the answer to this question. I could now give them his identity, Doreen McArthur and the sauna witnesses would confirm that I was indeed his double, I had alibis that would clear me personally of suspicion. If they published my photograph in the press they would catch him very quickly. I could leave out all stories of telepathy and account for my suspicions purely on the basis of the press description and knowledge of my brother's tendencies. Superintendant Montgomery might remember our last meeting, but if he remained sceptical I would only need to visit Doreen McArthur's pub or send her my photograph to convince him.

In other words, it was now within my power to clear up the strangler investigation immediately. By not doing so I was failing in my clear duty. I was making myself an accessory to any future crimes he might commit.

So why did I not act? The killer seemed to know the reason. Reckless as he was, he would surely not taunt me with something so vital to his personal safety unless he felt sure of me.

I do not think that I ever made any deliberate decision not to report him. I merely kept postponing it. And there were plenty of excuses for my delay: I wanted to spare my mother from any feeling of responsibility for his crimes; one did not lightly incriminate one's own flesh and blood; he had been so careless that he would probably get caught soon anyway – the latest photofit picture was accurate enough for some of my legal colleagues to make jocular comments about it. And as long as I could stop him from killing again, what harm was being done?

To the extent that there is a defensible reason for my delay, I think it relates to that last point. If I had saved Doreen's life, I could save any future potential victims. I think I resented the idea of police interference in what had become a personal struggle between us, a conflict between good and evil.

I agree in retrospect that this attitude displays a criminal degree of arrogance. But I was not consciously aware of it at the time. And there was growing evidence that I was making some headway in the battle.

As our mental communion continued to develop, I repeated my experiment of confronting him with the results of his crimes, of blasting him with further telepathic beams of recrimination. It was a public service activity that also gave me much pleasure. And, gradually, in the same way as I had been seduced by his evil pleasures, I found him becoming infected by my guilt. I also managed to impose on him something of my sense of caution, the ability to resist some of his foolhardy impulses.

His moods were somewhat cyclic, and there were times when the notion of a further killing came upon him. But I was always able to exert enough influence to make him back away. Several months passed without my having to handle any real crisis.

During this time my life returned almost to normal. I duly visited my doctor and he could not find anything physically wrong with me; I did not encourage him to investigate my mental state. I heeded my senior partner's advice and took Jean and the children for a fortnight's holiday in the south of France. While I was away, I experienced no mental contact with the killer, suggesting that there was indeed a geographical limit to our link. It was a welcome break. And on my return, things gradually settled down in the office and at home. The killer returned to my head, but I was now accustomed to the phenomenon and better able to control it. I was therefore able to proceed with my personal and professional life without too much suspicious behaviour.

The police continued their investigation, but without making any breakthrough. The killer had moved from his Portobello lodgings and was generally keeping a low profile. Gradually the topic became less prominent in the press. Edinburgh began to relax, though not entirely.

Then, in mid August, came the time of the annual Edinburgh Festival.

All summer the tourist season had been at its height. In the city centre, the street voices spoke with English or American accents, or didn't speak English at all. Every second person seemed to carry a camera. And among the visitors were many young women who had not learned to dread the historic corners of the Old Town, a prospect that the killer was finding more and more difficult to ignore.

At festival time the foreign invasion reached saturation level. And my mental leash on the killer broke under the strain.

TWENTY-TWO

W E ARRANGED TO MEET in the *Tolbooth Tavern*, near the eastern end of the Royal Mile. I am not sure whether he appreciated the significance of the location. The pub is part of the Tolbooth, a 16th Century building with pointed turrets and a prominent clock. The Tolbooth originally served as the Court House and prison for the old burgh of Canongate.

Considering its picturesque exterior, the bar was surprisingly ordinary inside. Possibly because of this, the locals had established a beachhead and were holding their own against the tourist tide. I bought myself a pint of beer and even managed to find a seat. In a back corner of the bar, a TV was showing horse racing, a welcome antidote to the cultural fever outside.

I didn't expect him to be punctual – that would not have been in character – but I knew he was on his way. I felt his mind fix on mine, as if I were transmitting a homing beacon, the signal growing gradually stronger as we approached our first physical conjunction. Then he was in the bar, had bought a drink and was across the table from me.

"Pleased to meet you, brother," he said, extending his hand.

Before I had time to think about it, I found I was shaking his hand. I let it go again and felt a shiver pass through my body. Was it entirely of revulsion? I am not sure. He sensed my feeling and laughed; I think he read it on my face as well as from my mind. "What's the matter?" he said. "Don't want to

160

be seen with the likes of me, is that it?"

"Yes."

"So why the big reunion? Why did you arrange to meet me?"

"I want to keep an eye on you. Make sure you behave yourself."

"Is that really what you want?"

"Absolutely."

He laughed again. "Never mind, we've got a good day for it."

"Good day for what?"

For a strangling, you stupid cunt. Look at those thousands of visitors outside. Who would notice one less? Maybe we could do one each.

God, you're disgusting.

"That's right, brother," he said aloud, lifting his drink to me. "And who knows me better than you?"

I had recognised within him that peculiar, intoxicating sense of excitement that usually preceded a killing. I found I both welcomed and dreaded it. I realised now how much I had been missing that feeling over the last few months, as if I were an addict whose drug supply had been cut off. But that was not my reason for meeting him. Surely he would not try to kill again with me physically present to restrain him?

And yet he had made no attempt to avoid me. He had welcomed my appearance, as a new element of excitement in his game.

As we sat across the table from each other our minds were never more united. I simultaneously saw through his eyes and mine, heard through his ears, shared all of his senses. As I looked into his face, that evil parody of my own, I saw, superimposed upon it, his view of my features. When one of us spoke, his voice rang with a ghostly mental echo. We became unaware of whether we were talking out loud or only inwardly. This was dangerous, as there was much in our conversation that we could not risk being overheard.

He finished off his drink in a single gulp. "Let's get out of this fucking place," he said.

"Why?"

"Why not? I'm bored. Come on, drink up."

As we were leaving, a man at the next table said, "Hey, are you two twins?"

"No," said my brother. "I'm the Canongate Stranger and this is my waxwork for Madame Tussauds. Lifelike, isn't it?"

I couldn't help laughing. The man looked puzzled, then resentful. "No offence. I only asked a civil question."

"Don't bother about him," I said. "He's got a peculiar sense of humour."

The man was still looking huffy as we left. When we emerged into the street, we were still laughing together at the joke. We walked slowly up the road, and I found myself being infected by his sense of adventure.

We were proceeding up the Royal Mile, in the section known as the Canongate. On either side of the narrow street were some of the oldest buildings of the Old Town, high tenement blocks of brown stone, punctuated by closes and alleys leading to remote back courts. It was half past one on a Wednesday afternoon, but the streets were so packed with people that it might have been Saturday. It was the second week of the Festival, and there was an atmosphere of excitement that strangely matched the killer's own, less innocent emotion.

Great place for a murder. What do you think?

You're joking.

Why not? They're the ones that dubbed me the Canongate Strangler, so what do they expect?

Fair enough. But there's one possible snag. What about the hundreds of people watching?

He laughed. He was quickly reaching an emotional high, and a fantasy scenario formed in his mind.

Murder Scenario No. 1. Roll up folks for the latest Festival Fringe event. Street theatre as you've never known it before. See the Canongate Strangler, in the middle of the street that bears his name, strangle a tourist for the amusement of the locals.

Performances liable to untimely interruption, as he will require to nip down the nearest pend at the sound of a two-tone siren.

How about that? Not bad, eh?
Might be a few practical difficulties.

As long as he was operating at this level of fantasy, I felt relaxed and free to share his mood. When more workable propositions entered his mind I would have to be on guard. And how could he manage one of those with half the population of Europe and America crowding us out of the city?

We carried on uphill, passing from the Canongate into the High Street. I pointed out John Knox's house but it didn't interest him. We reached a crossroads. Ahead of us the Mile carried on into the very heart of the city, past Parliament Square and St. Giles Cathedral on its road to the castle; on either corner, serving as incongruous portals to this route, the 17th Century Tron Church looked across the street at a Pizza Parlour.

"Let's cut down to Princes Street."

"Why?"

"We're getting too near my office."

"Oh, I see. Playing truant are you?"

"None of your business."

We turned to the right and crossed the bridge over the railway before resuming our westward route. Soon the wide cityscape of Princes Street Gardens and the castle opened out before us. Here the streets were busier still, the surrounding accents even more diverse. I felt secure and relaxed. He would have to wait long and go far to find a quiet enough corner for a killing. In contrast, he was growing more and more restless. We had been walking for more than fifteen minutes and he was not a patient man. He also wanted another drink. His desire to kill was even stronger, but here was a weakness to be exploited.

"Let's go to Rose Street."

"All right."

Rose Street. That long back lane where all the area's pubs had been tucked away out of respectable view, behind the main thoroughfares of the New Town. Here I could surely divert him down an alcoholic byway.

"I know what you're trying," he said. "It won't do any good."

"I only want another drink. Don't you want another drink?"

"Oh yes," he said, "and I'm going to have one. But your plan won't work."

Rose Street was just as crowded as elsewhere, and so were all the pubs we looked into. We eventually settled for *The Rose Street Brewery*, an old building where the proprietors brewed their own beer on the premises and served it in a dark, low-ceilinged lounge bar. It was no quieter here than elsewhere, but even I had grown tired of wandering. I squeezed my way to the counter and bought two pints of their home brew, which they called 'Auld Reekie.' It was a potent draught, which was bound to reduce his harmful potential. We looked in vain for an empty table and instead found a standing place at the centre of the bar, at a high round table made out of a large wooden barrel. It was a good vantage point from which to survey the field.

"Nice pint, isn't it?"

"It does the business."

"Is that all that matters?"

"Of course," he said. "I tell you what, since you like it so much, we'll come back here afterwards and get pissed." He laughed at my reaction and took a long drink, continuing to look round the bar for potential customers.

At first the outlook was not promising. There were plenty of eligible young women around, but they were all in company. Before long, I felt his impatience begin to mount again. He took another large gulp of his drink, ready to push on somewhere else.

I told you it would be no good.

Did you? I don't remember. Anyway, it's too soon to give up. We can move on in a minute.

Please yourself. It won't make any difference.

In fact, moving on would have suited my strategy very well. With each pub, and each hastily-downed drink, he would be less capable of mischief. And we would not run out of venues. There are few undertakings more debilitating than a pub crawl of Rose Street.

But it was not to be. At a table not far from us, two men and two women had been finishing off a bar lunch. Just then three of them got up and took their leave of the fourth, who was left sitting at the table on her own.

He was over there before I even had time to think about stopping him. "Mind if we sit here?"

"No, carry on."

She was an attractive black girl, probably in her early twenties. She wore a summer top and slacks and carried the usual guide book and camera. She glanced briefly up from her book as we sat down, then looked up again and took a longer retake.

"Hey," she said. "Are you two twins?"

"No," he said. "All us white folks look the same. Are you an American?"

He could have said this in a way that would have offended her. But instead he had brought out all his damnable charm. She laughed. "Touché. I suppose one's as obvious as the other. Are people always asking you that?"

"Pretty often."

Soon we were talking freely. Her name was Jackie Harris and she was a violinist with an American orchestra playing at the Festival. Her companions, who were fellow musicians, had gone off to see a play which she hadn't been interested in. She was intending to do some sightseeing instead. We introduced ourselves as Ted and Henry.

"I gather you're locals," she said.

"How did you work that out?"

She laughed again. "Oh, I don't know. I just somehow got that impression. What do you do?"

"Guess."

"I've no idea. Comedians, maybe."

"No. One of us is a lawyer and the other's unemployed. Any idea which?"

"Haven't a clue. Neither of you looks like a lawyer to me. I think you're both crazy."

"He's the lawyer."

"Is he? You don't have quite the same accent. Why is that?"

"We were brought up separately. We only found each other recently."

"Is that so? That's really nice."

"Isn't it?"

"You should be able to get your brother a job then."

"I don't think so. He's an uneducated bum."

"You *are* crazy. Both of you."

You've no idea how much, dear. I think we're on to a good thing here. I've always fancied strangling a darkie.

So you're a racist as well as a murderer?

Not at all. I look on all people equally.

You mean you regard them with equal contempt?

That's right. I just like a little bit of variety in my women. What's wrong with that?

You'll never get her alone. She's not a cheap tart that you can win over with your smooth talk.

Want a bet?

Anyway, you've still got me to reckon with.

I'm sure I'll work something out.

"Where were you thinking of going?" he asked her.

"I fancied seeing round the castle. I've been reading about it in my book."

"Why don't we come with you and show you round?"

"Do you know about the castle?"

"Absolutely bugger all. All right then, you can show us round."

She shook her head. "I've never met anyone like you two. I'm not sure if I'll be safe."

"I don't know about him," I said. "But you'll be safe with me. And I do know about the castle. We can show each other round."

"OK," she said. "It's a deal."

166

Murder Scenario No. 2. In a gloomy dungeon of the castle, formerly used as a torture chamber, the young American visitor bends over to look at one of the fearsome instruments of cruelty. Immediately, the killer pounces and squeezes away her last breath in that perfect, grisly setting. He places the body on the rack, her open mouth and staring eyes conveying just the right expression for someone in the process of being torn in two by sadistic inquisitors. Then the killer, pleased with his day's work, goes off for a pint. Later, a group of tourists comment on the realism of the tableau.

Shows how much you know about the castle. They don't have a torture chamber.
No torture chamber? What kind of bloody castle is that?
Also, the place is full of security guards. Not to mention a few hundred tourists.
Don't worry, we'll get round it. I like a challenge.
And what do you think I'll be doing?
That's entirely up to you.

TWENTY-THREE

W E APPROACHED THE CASTLE indirectly, across Princes Street Gardens, which are laid out on the site of a former loch at the foot of the castle rock. We were all in a happy mood, though for different reasons. Jackie was enjoying an innocent excursion with two handsome strangers; my brother was following the scent of the kill, undeterred by the horde of people crowding the gardens; my feelings were more difficult to explain.

The black castle rock, 400 feet high, more and more dominated our viewpoint as we approached its base. We took our time, walking around the gardens to look at the floral displays, investigating a marquee that was housing some form of fringe theatre, stopping at a booth to buy ice cream, spending some time at the bandstand, listening to an amateur orchestra. My brother grew a little impatient with this last item, but Jackie had taken a professional interest in the band and would not be deterred.

Jackie, like most strangers who are not used to it as their daily landscape, was finding the city impressive.

"This is really interesting," she said, consulting her guidebook as we eventually drew nearer to the base of the rock. "It says here that the rock was once a volcano."

My brother had a brief vision of flinging her body into a pool of molten lava, but even he realised that he was a few years too late for this. "I think it's quite safe now," I said.

My brother merely smiled. *Don't be so sure of that.*

We crossed a footbridge over the railway and turned left along a narrow dirt track between the railway line and the foot of the cliff, which was almost perpendicular at this point. Here there were fewer people around, and this gave a further stimulus to his imagination.

Murder Scenario No. 3. The killer is walking with his victim along the narrow track at the base of the castle rock. He hears the sound of a train approaching from Waverley Station. "Let's stop and wave to the passengers," he says. She smilingly agrees, touched by his innocent, friendly nature. As the train passes they wave to the passengers, some of whom wave back. Then he grabs her throat and begins to throttle her. At the train windows he sees the waving hands falter, the mouths drop open in disbelief. He cannot wave back now, his hands being fully engaged, but he treats the first class passengers to a conspiratorial wink as their carriage goes past. They have paid extra after all. Flinging aside the body of his victim, he unpockets a small aerosol can and spray-paints the words STRANGLER RULES in large block letters on the rock face. By the time the police arrive, after a frantic phone call from Haymarket Station, he is lost in the crowd and drinking a well-earned pint.

You seem to find killing a thirsty occupation.
You know me. Any excuse for a pint.
I don't think a jury would consider that motive a mitigating factor.
They're not going to get the chance.
There isn't a train coming.
We could wait. There's bound to be one soon.
And I bet you don't have a paint can with you.
That's true.
No forward planning, that's your problem.
Ridiculous as this latest fantasy was, I kept a careful eye on him. But a group of tourists was following only a few yards behind us, and just then several more appeared round the corner

in front. I relaxed again.

The track widened as we approached the easier slopes near the castle's entrance. Here the base of the cliff was set further back, with a more gentle, grass-covered gradient in between. Even more people were now in view, scattered about the grass, some sitting enjoying the sun, others taking short-cuts. In several places there were groups of children playing. No material for fantasies here.

"How do we get to the entrance?" asked Jackie.

"You mean you don't want to climb the rock?" asked my brother.

She laughed. "I can afford the entrance fee."

"It's up there," I said, pointing up the hill towards the castle esplanade, hidden behind the terraced seating erected for the Military Tattoo. "We'll have to carry on the way we're going for a bit and then double back."

We left the gardens and made our way up the Mound, towards the castle's more gradual eastern approach. Then we cut off to the right, up a close that led virtually to the castle entrance.

I immediately regretted the choice of route as we began to climb the narrow stone stairway and the sunlight was cut off by the buildings on either side. Ahead of us, the route proceeded through a tunnel beneath another building. For the moment, there was no-one else in sight and we were alone in a dark bywater, away from the bustle of the festival city. This was the sort of location to give a killer inspiration, and I felt his mind respond to it. I had been slightly ahead of the other two, but now drew back level with them, on the other side of Jackie from my brother.

Murder Scenario No. 4. In the dark passage beneath the building, the strangler is now alone with his victim. He quickly seizes the opportunity and soon her life is draining away under his cruel fingers. Suddenly, a group of tourists appear from the street above and hurry down to the rescue. What should he do? If he flees before she is dead, he will leave yet another witness who knows him well. With deadly calm he continues with his task, turning his back on the pursuers to hide his face, carefully gauging the length of the narrowing gap from the sound of their footsteps. Is she dead? He squeezes on a few moments longer, just to be sure. Then, as they are almost upon him, he runs off down the close to the street below. An old lady is walking along the pavement, blocking his way. With joyful savagery he flings her aside and is soon lost in the crowd.

We were now in the tunnel and still alone. I tensed myself, trying to interpret his soaring emotions. Was he still only fantasising? It was difficult to tell. Then, ahead of cue, with the victim still unmolested, a group of people left the street above and came down towards us.

Not going for a drink this time?

Of course. You can take that for granted.

You know, these mental pictures of yours are rather imaginative. A little too melodramatic for my liking, but quite poetic just the same.

I'm glad you appreciate them.

Mind you, it's easy enough when they're all inside your head. I'm sure you couldn't express them in words.

I'm not interested in words, only action.

"You two have gone real quiet again," said Jackie. "Are you telepathic or something?"

"You'd be surprised."

We reached the street above and were immediately part of the crowd on the approach to the castle. A few yards from the entrance, a soldier in full highland dress stood playing the bagpipes, easily making himself heard above the background noise of the busy street. Soon we were walking across the broad esplanade, the rostrum for the display of military music and gymnastics that was twice nightly packing in audiences from everywhere in the world except Edinburgh. On either side, the tiers of seats rose above our heads like the open wings of a gigantic bird of prey.

"Have you been to the Tattoo?" asked Jackie. "I believe

it's really something."

"No," I said. "But I've heard it. Everyone in Edinburgh has, especially those who live round about."

She looked at me a little uncertainly, but made no comment. "I'm going to it tonight," she said.

Oh no you're not.

Oh yes she is.

"You're better sticking to Mahler," I said, referring to the concert her orchestra was giving at the Usher Hall the following evening.

"I can enjoy all kinds of music," she said.

"Who the fuck cares?" said my brother suddenly. "It's all a load of shit."

Jackie looked a little alarmed by this, but my brother, realising that his mask had slipped for a moment, followed it up with one of his most charming smiles.

At the castle entrance proper, we bought tickets and made our way towards the narrow bridge spanning the dry moat in front of the gatehouse. On either side of the bridge, a soldier in the uniform of a highland regiment stood on sentry duty.

My brother, keen to dispel any sinister overtones of his outburst, decided to follow it up with a bit of clowning. He walked over to one of the sentries and examined him closely. The soldier stood so motionless that he could almost have been mistaken for a waxwork dummy. While standing directly in front of him, my brother turned round to Jackie and said loudly, "Do you think he would move if I tickled his balls?"

Unable to stop myself, I laughed uncontrollably. Jackie looked initially aghast, then joined me. The sentry, true to his training, remained impassive. Jackie quickly recovered, looked embarrassed and hurried across the bridge to the castle gate, with me on her heels. My brother paused, partly extended his hand as if about to carry out his threat, then ran after us.

When we were safely across the drawbridge and through the gate, we proceeded for a few yards further, then stopped. We clung to each other, overcome by laughter.

When she had recovered, Jackie said, "I can't make you

two out at all. You're both crazy. You don't seem to give a damn about your national heritage, or about anything at all. You're like a couple of kids."

"It keeps us young."

"Sometimes I think Henry's got more sense – or are you Ted? I keep getting confused."

"Guess."

"But I think one of you is really as bad as the other."

"He's the bad guy."

"No, he is."

She shook her head. "You'd think twins would grow out of playing that sort of game. But I suppose you two haven't had the chance before."

For fuck's sake, don't tell me she's an amateur psychologist.

But she was not being seriously critical, and all three of us remained in a merry mood as we made our way up the winding approach road to the top of the rock. Several guides in green jackets and tartan trousers were taking round groups of tourists, explaining the historical significance of the various parts of the castle; it is partly a misnomer to call it a castle, as it is really a disparate collection of buildings dating from the 12th Century to early in the present one, representing the rock's successive functions as military defensive position, royal residence, army barracks and tourist attraction. We followed one of the guides for a while, then decided to go on our own, as Jackie was able to do just as well from her guidebook.

We spent an hour mingling with the crowds and experiencing the various delights that the castle had to offer. Jackie continued to be alternately appalled and delighted by our antics and our irreverent attitude to history. But in the main she was enjoying herself greatly, unaware that since entering the front gate she had been strangled to death half a dozen times, and that her corpse had been left desecrating the altar of St. Margaret's Chapel, guarding the Scottish Crown Jewels, hidden in the shadows of the stone archway at Foog's Gate, as an inmate of the Military Prison, graphically commemorating the dead in the War Memorial, and in attendance at the birthplace of King James VI, in the apartments of his mother, Mary Queen of Scots. All of these imaginary crimes occurred in locations filled with people, and I allowed none of them to affect my continuing mood of abandon.

Then we found ourselves at the head of a stairway that seemed to lead outwards, below the battlements overlooking Princes Street. "I don't think we've been down here," said my brother. "What is it?"

Jackie consulted her book. "It says it leads to the Western Defences," she said. "They seem to be battlements built at a lower level. They were originally intended to guard against enemies climbing up the western face of the rock, because it isn't quite so steep there."

It was now late afternoon. The sky had become overcast, with rain threatening, and the crowds were thinning a little. I looked down the stone steps and they were empty of people. My brother was continuing on an emotional high, but I picked up a subtle change in his mood, a hardening of resolve. I tried to distance myself from our joint euphoria, re-introduce an element of caution. I pointed to a notice that warned visitors of the number of steps and the exposed nature of the area.

"Maybe we should give it a miss," I said. "It looks as if it's going to rain."

"Don't be daft," he said. "That notice is for wheelchair cases."

"I'd like to go down," said Jackie. "Come on, we're all young and fit."

Having been outvoted, I made no further protest and followed them down the steps. The stairway remained enclosed for a short distance, then continued out in the open. I saw that, between the castle wall and the top of the rock face, there was a steep but climbable grass-covered slope, and that we were now on an open battlement enclosing this area and forming a broad arc along the edge of the precipice. At the foot of the steps, where the wall changed direction, the junction was marked by a stone sentry box with a domed roof. We carried on past this, down another short flight of steps and soon were at our greatest distance from the rest of the castle, with the main battlements far above us. Ahead was another sentry box where the route turned back towards the castle. Only a low wall separated us from the cliff whose base we had skirted earlier in the afternoon. We were now exposed to the full force of the wind and there was a trace of rain in the air. There was not another human being in sight, apart from the remote crowd in the castle above and the even more distant horde in the city below. This was a dangerous place.

Murder Scenario No. 11. While his victim is leaning over the wall, admiring the panoramic view of Princes Street and the New Town, the killer sneaks up behind her and puts his strong hands to work. What should he do with the body? Stuff it into the sentry box, a nice macabre surprise for the next splinter group of visitors? No, that would be too far to drag the corpse. Instead, he heaves her over the top of the wall and down the cliff. Just in case she wasn't quite dead, that should make certain. By the time the shaken onlookers below have recovered enough to raise the alarm, he is safely mingling again with the crowd in the castle. When the sirens are heard he is contemplating the choice of pubs in High Street.

This was the most plausible one so far. Just then Jackie, right on cue, stopped and leaned over the wall. "You get some view from here," she said, lifting her camera. My brother was standing directly behind her. I was a few yards away. Was he about to act at last? I was picking up the broadcast from his mind at full strength, but couldn't quite decide whether or not he was still only fantasising. The border between fact and fiction had become blurred. Then he moved closer to her, placing a hand on each shoulder. She didn't move. For an age they seemed frozen in that position, like a moving film that has been stopped at a single frame. I stood where I was, for the moment unable to move. His hands moved inwards a fraction.

Then he leaned forward and whispered in her ear. I could

not have made them out through my ears alone, but I picked up
the conversation clearly via his mind.

"Let's lose him," he said, "and go off somewhere on our
own."

She sighed. "Look," she said, "I've been having a great
afternoon. Don't spoil it, Ted. Or is it Henry?"

"Never mind which. I'm the one who knows how to please
a lady."

"I'm sure you do. But not this one, OK?"

She shook herself free and walked on ahead. He made no
resistance and followed on behind her. I felt a distinct sense of
anti-climax. Was it relief? Partly so at least.

So you chickened out, did you?

I'd no intention of doing anything here.

That's what you say.

We can be seen from above.

I hadn't noticed.

Anyway, someone could come along here at any moment.

*Nobody has so far. You could have had her there. I think
you're losing your nerve.*

*You can think what you fucking well like. Anyway, if I'd
had a go, what would you have done about it?*

*That's a good question. Wouldn't you like to know the
answer?*

We passed the other sentry box and were soon climbing
the steps back up to the safety of the main castle complex. The
crowd of tourists was now definitely thinner. The crisis was
over for the moment, perhaps for good.

"What do you want to do now?" my brother asked. "Will
we go for a drink?"

"I wouldn't mind," said Jackie, "But I want to keep in good
shape for the Tattoo."

"You'd enjoy it better drunk."

She laughed. "You Scots are a crowd of alcoholics," she
said. "Maybe I'll have just one." She had stopped and was
having another look at her guidebook. "Wait a minute, there's
something we've missed. We haven't been down to the castle

vaults."

"What are they? Is that where they store the beer?"

"According to this, it's where they now keep the 15th Century seige gun called Mons Meg. They took it down from the battlements because the weather was affecting the metal. So it says here, anyway."

"Let's go and see it then."

We went down the steps leading to the vaults, a series of large cellars underneath the buildings on the highest part of the castle rock. Not far inside the entrance stood a shirt-sleeved security guard with a walkie-talkie radio, and several groups of people still wandered around. It seemed safe enough.

The Mons Meg display was in two adjoining chambers, with stone walls and a high, curved ceiling. Each room had a separate entrance into the main corridor. In one of them the gun itself was displayed, and in the other there were periodical showings of a film about its history. We spent some time admiring the huge medieval cannon, then heard the soundtrack of the film as it began next door.

"Let's go in and watch the film."

"OK."

The only lighting in the chamber we now entered was from its two doorways and from the image on the screen. At first I could see nothing at all, and when our eyes got used to the dark the situation was not much improved. It appeared, however, that we were the only people in the audience.

Murder Scenario No. 12. The killer is alone with his victim in the pitch-black chamber of the castle vaults. Utilising his superb sense of touch, he quickly does his business. He starts to drag the body to the blackest corner of the room, where it will probably not be discovered until it begins to smell. Then he has a much, much better idea. An inspiration. Temporarily abandoning his charge, he looks into the adjoining room. There is no-one there and the magnificent siege gun stands alone in its glory. Quickly he goes back for the corpse, drags it through the doorway and stuffs it head first down the barrel of the

177

cannon. As he strolls away, he imagines the next day's headlines: *American Violinist Becomes Human Cannonball,
Murdered Musician in Mons Meg Maw—*

That's the most ridiculous fantasy yet.
What do you mean? I've already started.
It was true. In that black vault, as our joint adventure
reached its ecstatic climax, our minds were united as never
before, and we almost seemed to occupy the same body. It
might have been my hands that encircled her throat, my legs
that accepted the kicks from her diminishing death struggle. As
if it had been planned that way, the film co-operated with a
particularly noisy piece of sound track.

Together we stood at the top of that wonderful summit,
growing ever taller as we absorbed her life-force.

Then it was over and we had a body on our hands.
Now look what you've done!
How can I? You can't see a damn thing in here.
*Why did you have to go and kill her? It was only a joke.
Why did you actually have to do it?*
*You know perfectly well. You're playing with the big boys
now. You should know what that means.*
It's not fair. Let's get out of here quick.
Not yet. Have you forgotten the plan?
*You're crazy! Leave her here. We'll be well away before
they find her.*
*Where's your sense of adventure? Go in next door and
check if the coast's clear.*
But—
*Do what you're fucking well told! We're in this together
now.*
All right, all right!
In the adjoining room, three tourists were admiring the
cannon. There was no sign of the security guard.
There are people here. Let's get out now.
*Hang on a moment and see if they go. Pretend to look at
the gun and let me know when they're away.*

What if they go next door?
What would be the point? The film's finished.

The tourists seemed to linger on for an age, and there were further angry mental altercations between my brother and me. Eventually, however, the visitors made their way out into the corridor.

That's them away.
Right, come through here and give me a hand.
This is madness.
Come on!
Where are you?
"Over here."
Keep your voice down!

Together we carried the body to the doorway. Then, after checking that the adjoining chamber was still empty, we carried her over to Mons Meg.

You hold her legs while I try to get the head in.

We slowly eased her, head first, into the mouth of the cannon. It was a tight fit, but we managed without too much trouble. Her toes finished up a couple of inches from the end, barely tucked out of sight.

Right. Now we can get the fuck out of here.

Wait. We can't let the security guard see us together. He might remember seeing twins at the scene of the crime.

You're right. You go first and I'll follow in a moment.

We did this and got safely past the security guard, who didn't appear to pay us any attention. We met again on the downhill road to the castle gate, along with the other departing visitors.

Well, that was a good afternoon's work. Let's go for a pint.
How can you be so casual? That poor girl's dead.
I hope so. We're in trouble if she isn't.
And she was supposed to be playing tomorrow night.
So they'll play with one violin short. I'm sure no-one'll notice the difference.
And putting her into that cannon. That was really sick.
Yes, I thought that was a nice touch. It's a pity they don't

use it for the one o'clock salute. They could have fired her through the front window of Marks & Spencer.

It's not funny. It's not funny at all. It was only a game and you spoiled it.

Of course it was only a game. But the stakes are high.

We proceeded down Castlehill and into Lawnmarket. After considering several pubs, we went into *Deacon Brodie's Tavern*, named after the infamous 18th Century villain, who was a respectable councillor by day and leader of a gang of criminals by night.

Well, cheers brother. It's a pity we didn't grow up together. We could have had great fun.

No we couldn't. I'm finished with you. I never want to see you again.

I told you before, we're in this together now. There's no going back.

Our dialogue continued in a similar vein. Presently, we heard the sound of a police siren in the street outside.

EDITOR'S INTERPOLATION

AT THIS POINT Cunningham's manuscript becomes somewhat incoherent. In the ten or so pages that follow, the surprisingly high standard of literacy he has shown so far suddenly takes a dip, with extended examples of appalling grammar, spelling and punctuation – in fact much more in keeping with the style one would expect from a man of his social and educational background. If that were the only problem, something might still have been made of the passage, but a mere translation into good English would not be enough to put right what can only be described as the delirious ravings of a madman.

This part of the manuscript has therefore been omitted. The final chapters, where Cunningham regains something of his previous form, have been retained in full, with only minor corrections.

So far as any sense can be made of the deleted passage, the following elements emerge:–

(1) There are several expressions of profound guilt about the murders in general and that of Jackie Harris in particular. These are interspersed with contrasting episodes of callous defiance, which could almost have been written by a different person.

(2) The narrator seems to have been ill during the period described, having apparently suffered a nervous breakdown.

The above should be enough to allow the reader to pass on to this strange story's even more extraordinary denouement. It is left up to him to decide whether any real light has been shed upon the enduring mysteries of the case.

TWENTY-FOUR

IT IS ONLY with the greatest difficulty that I can bring myself to write this final part of my narrative. This is due not only to the subject matter but also to my mental state at the time. My pathetic failure to prevent the murder of Jackie Harris was followed by a nervous collapse – judging by the immediately preceding pages, writing about it has caused a relapse – and I had only partially recovered at the time of the episode I am now about to recount. No doubt because of this, my recollection is incomplete and confused in places, though I remember the important parts with a terrifying clarity. I believe it was about a month after the castle murder. At any rate, it immediately preceded my arrest and incarceration.*

I still can hardly believe that he managed to pull off such an unexpected *tour de force*. Nor is it easy, after our almost comradely outing together, to come to terms with the fact that he could contemplate an act of such malice towards me. But it should not really be surprising. The depth of his evil is a matter of public record, not least in these pages. And I know that he had grown to hate me. Because of me, he had, for the first time in his wicked life, known the bitter taste of repentance; the burden of conscience, the restrictions of responsibility, the tortures of self-recrimination, were all unwelcome novelties that I had introduced to him. In return for participating in his pleasure, I had made him share my pain. And his nature is not a forgiving one.

---

* That was on October 5 — ED.

182

It was seldom these days that we could achieve any moments of individual mental privacy. His presence had become part of the background furniture of my mind, though for the most part I was barely aware of it. Even so, had I not been asleep at the time, he could not have caught me so completely off-guard.

As I said above, my recollection is not complete. But the main events in that morning's drama still act and re-enact themselves in my mind, with an almost hallucinatory quality —

I have been sleeping late – a common occurrence these days – and my brain is in a pleasant, free-wheeling state as it slowly comes to life. I gradually become aware that he is already awake and about some kind of business; that he is in a public place, engaged in conversation with someone. For a while, as the last mists of sleep are still clearing, I listen to the conversation and look at the face opposite him without the significance registering. Then the words begin to acquire meaning.

" —another scone?"

"No thanks, I feel quite full. I had a good breakfast before I came out."

"Another cup of coffee then?"

"Yes, all right."

He calls over the waiter and orders two coffees.

"So you're feeling much better now?"

"Yes, I think the worst is over."

"It's good to see you looking so well. We've all been really worried about you."

"All of you?"

"What do you mean?"

"You as well?"

"Yes, of course. Why do you ask that?"

"Don't you know?"

"No."

"I don't care about the others. But I'm glad you feel that way."

The girl looks at him uncertainly, as if puzzled and a little embarrassed by the comment. There is a pause, then she says, "You still haven't said why you wanted me to meet you here."

"Do you need a reason?"

Her uncomfortable look returns. "No, but— "

"I just wanted to see you. What's wrong with that?"

"Nothing, it's just— When you phoned this morning I wasn't sure what to think. I didn't want to refuse."

"I'm glad you didn't."

"But it still doesn't seem— Are you sure you're all right?"

"Yes, of course. You just said you thought I looked well. Didn't you mean it?"

"Yes but— you know what I mean Mr. Middleton, with you being so ill and everything— "

"I know, but I'm fine now, Valerie. All the better for seeing you again. And there's no need to be so formal any more. You can call me Ted."

Valerie! Oh my God!

Suddenly I am awake.

You bastard, you rotten, vicious, evil, malicious bastard!

Oh good morning, brother. Enjoy your long lie?

What are you doing with that girl?

What do I usually do with nice young girls?

You can't, oh Christ you mustn't, you vindictive swine, I won't let you!

Yes, I had an idea that you fancied her. Now I'm certain.

I am being impersonated! But how can she possibly mistake him for me? There may be a facial resemblance, but how can he pass himself off as an educated man, a lawyer with whom she has been working closely for more than two years? I realise that he must have been learning as much from my mind as I have from his. And of course, in the present context, he is not having to demonstrate any particular legal aptitude. Only his well-tried conversational skills.

"How have you been managing without me?"

"Oh, there's been plenty for me to do. I've been helping Mr. Moffat keep up with your work, and there's always lots of copy work in the typing pool."

"That's not what I meant. I wasn't asking about the office. I was asking about you."

Valerie seems to be growing increasingly embarrassed. "Oh, I'm all right."

"Aren't you pleased to see me?"

"Yes— Mr. Middleton, why did you want to meet me? I should be at work. I know you're my boss and everything, but— "

"Never mind the bloody office. It's managed without me for a month. It can manage without you for a day."

"A day?"

"Yes, the weather's nice. I thought we might go for a walk somewhere. It would do me a lot of good."

No Valerie, for God's sake don't do it, go back to the office, get away from him!

Shut up. She can't hear you.

"I'm not sure," she says. "It doesn't seem right, Mr. Middleton."

"Ted. Why not? You're a beautiful girl, Valerie. I've always liked you a lot. Don't you like me just a little bit?"

Valerie's face has gone red. "Mr. Middleton— Ted— you're a married man."

"Don't remind me. To tell you the truth, Valerie, my wife and I haven't been getting on too well lately."

And whose fault's that?

"She's been no help at all to me while I've been ill. She doesn't understand what I've been going through."

You bloody liar. She loves me and she's been worried sick about me.

Who's talking about you?

"Yes, Valerie. It looks as if we might be heading for a divorce."

"Oh, I'm really sorry to hear that Mr.— Ted."

"It's just one of these things. Anyway, I would really appreciate it if you could keep me company for a while. Just as a friend. I won't bother you or do anything to embarrass you. And I'll fix it with the office."

"Well, if you put it like that—"

Until now, I have been too panic stricken to think constructively about the situation. His intentions are apparent; they would have been clear from his past form, even without my ability to read his mood. What can I do? I managed to stop him from killing once before, purely by mental interference. But it was a close thing, and now he will be prepared, better able to resist me. I can try that as a last resort, but cannot risk it as my only strategy. I will have to try and reach them physically. He won't be able to keep his location from me this time. I now read his mind too well.

He is aware of that, of course. He knows I am bound to interfere. And he welcomes it. A contest with me will give him that additional thrill which he forever craves. So will making Valerie his next victim.

I am still trying to work out where they are. My vision is of course confined to the view through his eyes and he will not move his head around at my command, allow me to see more of the place. This is not just because he wants to make things difficult for me: his attention is fixed on the face of the girl sitting opposite him. Still, I have picked up enough to gather that they are in some kind of up-market coffee house. It has a low ceiling, red bench seats, theatre and concert posters and, on the wall opposite him, a large antique dresser with a mirror and a row of antiquarian books that are for sale. The voices at the next table have American accents. I don't know the place, but reckon that it cannot be far from the city centre. It has the feel of somewhere in the heart of the tourist web.

There is no point in leaving home before I know their precise location, and they don't seem to be in any hurry to move. I get out of bed and quickly prepare to go out. Just as I have finished, they rise from the table and he goes over to pay the bill. I see a little more of the coffee house – a low counter, glass cases containing fudge and home-baked scones, a back wall of bilious green, decorated with brown silhouettes of historical figures, like the victims of some ancient atomic blast. Still not enough to identify the place.

Are you ready to follow us now? Good.
Still think this is all a game, don't you?
Of course.

As soon as they reach the street, I recognise the location. They are in the Royal Mile. In the Canongate, only a few yards from the Tolbooth, the site of our last rendezvous. He seems determined to live up to his nickname.

"Where do you want to go?" Valerie asks.

"We could have a walk in Holyrood Park. It's not very far."

"That's a good idea."

Valerie now seems much more relaxed and reconciled to the outing. I have mentioned earlier my occasional fantasies about getting personally involved with her, and how easy I thought it would be. It now looks as if he is proving me fatally right. She is only dressed for the office, in blouse, skirt and a light overcoat, but as she looks into my eyes and smiles – into *his* eyes, the ones she thinks are mine – it seems to me that she has never looked more attractive. I become overcome by emotion, unable to act.

Nice, isn't she? I must say, you've got good taste.

I resist the urge to respond. I cannot afford to get drawn into a mental slanging match with him. It will only serve his purpose by upsetting me further, impairing my ability to act effectively.

Handicapped by the usual double set of sense impressions, I make my way out into the street. Then I stop and try to exercise more mental control. Being now much more used to the phenomenon, I have acquired the technique of toning down his input, making it subservient to the immediate reality about me. With his homicidal fever broadcasting at full strength, it is a little more difficult, but eventually I manage.

I pass a telephone box and briefly consider phoning the police. I quickly dismiss the idea. If I convince them at all, it is unlikely I will do so in time to prevent the murder; if I galvanise them into any kind of action, it is as likely to be aimed in my direction as the killer's, and that is something I dare not risk. I cannot even afford the time for the phone call. He has a start on me of half the city.

I have only been walking for a hundred yards or so when I see a Hackney cab and flag it down.

"Where to?" the driver asks.

I hesitate. Valerie and the killer are now walking down the Canongate, in the direction of Holyrood Palace. If I can guess their ultimate destination, I might be able to cut them off. On the other hand, as soon as he realises my intention, he is liable to change direction and try to lose me. It is better to play safe, even at the risk of getting caught in the city centre traffic.

"The junction of High Street and the Bridges," I tell the driver. "I'll direct you from there."

We start on our way. Within a few moments we are stopped by a red light. This proves to be the beginning of a trend. As the mid-morning traffic builds up, my frustration grows with it. The killer picks this up. He has my mental input turned well down, but occasionally gives it a boost, just for his sadistic pleasure. By the time I am through my second set of lights, they have reached the end of the Royal Mile and are standing at the entrance of Holyrood Palace. They look through the metal gates at the stately courtyards and towers, a guaranteed vortex for sucking in visitors. But locals are made of stronger stuff.

"Have you ever seen through the Palace?" he asks her.

"No."

"And you've lived in Edinburgh all your life!"

"So have you. Have you ever been in?"

"No."

They both laugh. "Do you want to go in now?" he asks.

"Not particularly. Do you?"

"No. I'd rather enjoy the fresh air. I tell you what, why don't we climb Arthur's Seat."

"Oh come on. That's going a bit too far. In these shoes?"

"They're not high heels."

"They're not exactly climbing boots either."

"We can go up the footpath for a bit. If the going gets rough, we can always go back."

"Oh, all right then. Just for part of the way."

Valerie doesn't need much persuading. She looks as though she is beginning to enjoy her day off work; after all, being in the company of her boss, there can be no comeback.

Arthur's Seat. The highest of the group of hills in the middle of Holyrood Park. Not the most densely populated part of the city, particularly on a midweek autumn morning, after the tourist season has begun to wane. It is also an area where any pursuer can only follow on foot. I am not sure whether he has earlier managed to hide his plan from me, or whether it is a brilliant improvisation. But now it doesn't need a mind reader to see what it is.

They cross the road that encircles the hills, begin to climb a steep footpath on the nearest slope. I am halfway there and stuck in another traffic queue.

I give the taxi driver new instructions. "I want to go to Holyrood Park. You can bypass High Street, if that'll get us there sooner."

"It might have, if you'd told me earlier."

"I didn't know before— I mean, I hadn't made my mind up."

"Which part of the park do you want?"

I try to remember the route of the footpath they are following; I do not think it is on Arthur's Seat itself, but on one of the lesser hills, and I may be able to cut them off. But it is many years since I have been there and I am not sure. It would be a disastrous short-cut that left us separated by an unclimbable cliff. I have to find a path that will lead to them. And the only one I am certain of is the one they are on.

"Queens Drive, just round from the Palace," I tell the driver. "As quickly as you can."

He mutters something I cannot make out and does a U-turn at the first opportunity. This taxi driver does not seem like the type who is very tolerant of his passengers' eccentricities.

Anyway, trying to cut them off will make no difference. He knows all my movements. And already they are alone. He can kill her now if he wants, but he is not ready. He is enjoying the chase. He wants me to get nearer, so I can properly join in his game.

The footpath they are climbing winds up and around the hill, roughly in parallel to the road below. A shifting panorama of the city grows beneath them, becoming ever wider in its sweep the higher they climb. I sit back in the taxi and shut my eyes. The view through his eyes sharpens and fills out. Now every detail of the city is laid out below me on this clear autumn morning, and Valerie is by my side, innocently enjoying the walk to her death. I try to probe his mind more deeply, looking for something that will help me. I find only what I already know. His transparent intention; that now familiar mood, growing ever stronger as it nears its fulfilment, its unbearable, unthinkable climax. My own feelings escalate in reaction to his, to an opposing peak.

Don't be sick in the taxi, brother. The driver might throw you out.

Don't answer him. Mustn't let him bait me. I put a mute on his revolting thoughts, concentrating on his visual input, trying to keep a check on their position. The track continues its upward spiral, laying bare another, larger section of Edinburgh with every few yards. On their left they are skirting the foot of a low, rugged cliff, the Salisbury Crags, encircling the brow of the hill like a crown of thorns. From time to time red metal notices warn them of falling rocks. If only that was the full extent of her danger!

"I've never been up here before," says Valerie. "You can almost see the whole city."

"It's even better at the top."

"Have you been there?"

"No, but it's bound to be, isn't it?"

She laughs. "You know, Ted," she says, still hesitating at the unaccustomed use of his Christian name, but less so than before, "you've changed lately. I've always liked— always liked working for you, but recently you've been different. You seem less formal, to have loosened up a bit."

"So I'm a loose man. Are you a loose woman."

"Now now. Remember your promise."

"Don't worry Valerie, you're safe with me."

"I wonder what they're doing in the office just now? Probably typing some boring old title deeds. At least your work's a bit more interesting than that stuff."

Yes Valerie, talk about work. Show up his ignorance. You know I've got a double, you've met him before. For God's sake, get away from him.

That's right, brother. Let off some steam. It'll do you good.

He is right. Even if she were able to hear me, she cannot escape from him now. But my explosive frustration needs release. Ignoring his taunts, I continue to simmer, biding my time.

"Don't talk about work," he says to her. "Let's forget it for a day."

"All right. I don't mind."

They are almost at the top of the hill. They pause for breath and look back to admire the view. From here, the city's historic centre is buried in a mundane townscape of council estates and industrial buildings; the gothic spires compete for attention with modern tower blocks, the castle rock is an insignifaicant wart. Here he is far removed from the reminders of tradition, the trappings of civilisation; he can look down with contempt on the tiny people far below and their petty rules of behaviour. With each breath of the cold air, he inhales renewed vigour, a new sense of purpose. Up here he is above them all. Here anything is permitted.

Oh, get away from him Valerie, run for your life! He's in a dangerous mood!

Calm down brother, I'm not ready yet. I want you to have a ringside seat.

They begin walking again and she is safe for the moment. Where are they now? I must keep track of their position. The taxi has stopped again. More traffic lights! They are at the top of the hill and the path is running level. Soon it will dip again and I will have a better view of what lies ahead. What's the matter with these lights? Will they never change?

"Wake up, sir. We're here."

191

"What?" I open my eyes. I am in Holyrood Park. Alongside the road is the hill they are climbing, a few yards away the flight of steps at the foot of the track they have been following. Quickly I get up and open the door.

"That'll be three pounds twenty, sir."

"What? Oh yes, just a minute. Here you are."

"Have you nothing smaller?"

"No— I don't know. Keep the change."

"Thank you very much, sir."

I slam the taxi door and start running, grateful for the release into physical activity. Just as I reach the bottom of the footpath, they begin to descend the other side of the hill. I stop and shut my eyes, take a check on their position. Before them is an entirely new panorama. Ahead is Arthur's Seat, the highest hill in the group, the highest point of the city. Between it and the hill they have climbed, the track dips into a valley, almost joining the surrounding road which turns up to meet it. If I had stayed in the taxi, I could have met them at the bottom. I curse and begin my climb, the killer's laughter echoing in my mind. Did he know about this, did he hesitate before the top of the hill, just to lead me into my fatal error? Or is this just another example of his infernal luck?

Once more seeing through two pairs of eyes, I stumble and almost fall. I realise that it would have made no difference. If he had seen me coming up towards him, he would have stopped and done the business right there, presenting me on arrival with the corpse of my secretary. Some such gesture is still his plan. Trying to pull myself together, I thrust the killer's mental input to the back of my mind and concentrate on the path before me. Very soon I am out of breath. My illness has left me out of condition. But still my progress is quicker than their casual stroll. Before long I will catch up with them.

"Race you to the bottom," the killer says suddenly, and begins to run down the hill away from her. A moment later I hear her running on behind, no doubt taken by surprise, but now joining in the game.

"Wait for me."

She chases him down the hill, as if they are two children playing. When he reaches the bottom, I have again stopped for breath, the greater part of the hill still in front of me. There is a pain in my side and my clothes are soaking with sweat. If I ever do catch up with them, I will have no strength to interfere. He waits for Valerie as she scrambles down the last few yards of the rough slope, and catches her at the foot. She makes no move to pull herself free as they stand there, laughing together and catching their breath.

"Really Ted. You're like a big schoolboy."

"Just because I won."

"You had a start."

"You're younger than me. You could have caught up."

"You're mad, you really are. What do we do now?"

"Let's climb up there, right to the top."

"You *are* mad!"

"Come on, it's not exactly Mount Everest."

"It's high enough. I'm not dressed for it."

"Yes you are. Look, there's a track over there. Come on, follow me."

"Oh, all right then. But if it gets too rough, I'm going back."

"It'll be OK."

So proceeds the cat and mouse game he is playing with me. By the time I have dragged my rebelling body to the top of the first hill, they are well on their way up the second. For the first time, I can see them with my own eyes, two tiny figures on the green and brown mottled slope, an impossible distance away. Then they vanish round a corner in the track. I despair for a moment, then regain my resolve. Now I can go downhill for a while, get a rest, bridge some of the gap. If only I had not rushed at the hill, taken it more steadily, as they did. I have used up my energy, while they are still comparatively fresh.

My bodily energy, perhaps, but not my strength of purpose. I must stop this abomination. I will save Valerie, even if I kill myself in doing so.

Aware of my progress, he is setting a strong pace. "Steady

on," she says, as he pushes on along the narrow track. "You'd think there was someone after us."

"Maybe there is."

"Don't be silly. Slow down a bit."

He stops and takes her hand to help her up the next part of the slope. She arrives abreast of him, but doesn't let go, and they proceed hand in hand until the narrowness of the track forces them into single file again. I imagine myself in his place, treating it as the innocent outing she imagines it to be. In the context of the present horror, this vision of what might have been has an unbearable poignancy. What is mere marital infidelity, compared with his purpose? Tears fill my eyes, mingling with the sweat. His viewpoint takes over as mine blurs, and I stumble and fall, hitting my knee on a rock.

I pause for a moment, nursing the pain and wiping my eyes. Then I start on again at a steadier pace. There is no point in hurrying. The three of us are alone on the hills. He can kill her at any time. He will let me get as near as he wants me to, no more and no less. My best plan is to conserve what strength I have and hope that he miscalculates. The track is much narrower than the one on the other hill, travelling in a wide zig-zag to catch the easiest part of the slope, occasionally having rough wooden steps built in to help the climb. From time to time I get a feeling of *déjà vu* from a distinctive piece of rock or turn of the path that I have earlier seen through his eyes. I have now found my optimum rate. My heart has stopped racing and the pain has receded to a bearable background. There is still half of the hill between us, but though the gap is no longer narrowing, it is not widening either.

"I'm exhausted," says Valerie. "Let's stop for a moment."

"All right."

They have now reached the top of the path; from here on the slope becomes even steeper, the ground more rocky, and there is no properly defined track. They sit together on a rock, looking back down the way they have come. They can now see beyond the first hill to the sea. Most of the city is now out of sight on the other side of the hill; its affairs are remote, its tiny inhabitants now invisible. But one other human being *is* in view.

"Look," says Valerie. "There's someone coming up the track behind us."

"So there is."

"Maybe he's following us."

"I think he is."

"Come on, you're not serious. He just wants to climb the hill as well."

"Maybe."

"He looks a bit like you."

"Maybe it's my double."

"I'd forgotten about him. Did you ever find out who he is?"

"Yes, he's my twin brother."

"You're kidding!"

"No, it's true."

"I didn't know you had a twin."

"Neither did I, until he showed up."

"But how is that possible?"

"I was adopted. My parents only took one of us."

"And they didn't tell you about him? That's an amazing story. Have you met him yet?"

"Yes."

"What's he like?"

"You've seen him. He looks just like me."

"You know what I mean. What sort of person is he?"

"He's a bastard!"

He declares this so vehemently that she is unsure how to react. They both look down at their pursuer. We see each other through one another's eyes, two small figures, one with a companion. The gap between them growing inexorably smaller.

"I wonder if it is him?" she asks.

"It is."

"You can't tell properly from here. Why on earth would he want to follow us?"

"I don't know, but I'm glad he did."

"Why?"

"So that I can throw him over a cliff. Come on, let's get going again."

She seems puzzled by his answer, and a little uneasy. They resume their climb in silence for a while. Their stop has narrowed the gap a little, but soon I am myself compelled to rest. I cut it as short as my body will let me and doggedly resume. By the time I have reached the end of the path, they are almost at the rocky summit. There are two peaks, one having a small stone pedestal with a round top, like a sundial. He climbs up to it, then pulls her up the few remaining yards to the small concrete platform. They stand together, catching their breath and taking in the view. She makes no move to let go of his hand. A cold wind blows against them, but for the moment, their bodies overheated by the climb, it is just what they need. As they take in the 360 degree panorama, it seems as if half of Scotland is laid out before them: the Firth of Forth along the northern horizon, the great metal girders of the railway bridge plainly visible; the Pentland Hills on the south; the urban spread of Edinburgh and its lesser neighbours filling the spaces between. To him, the location is symbolic: for the moment he stands taller than any man in the city, he is its greatest citizen, he is stripped bare of its tiresome rules. He is ready for his grandest gesture. No more for him the furtive crime, hastily executed in anonymous darkness. His ultimate act of defiance, his unchallengeable claim of superiority will take place at midday, in view of the entire community that has vainly hunted him for nearly a year. To me, he is beaming his plan from the city's highest broadcasting tower. His companion is not intended to descend from that peak alive.

Oh Valerie, get away from him now, run, jump, roll down the hill, any minor injury is worth the risk, distance yourself, don't stand with him on that deadly summit. I try to shout a warning, but the wind blows away what little breath I have left.

Get a move on brother, you're holding up the show.

I am doing my best. I am now virtually running up the

slope, sliding on the damp vegetation, almost falling into ruts, frantically waving my hands in warning. "Look," says Valerie, "he's really going some. He seems to be trying to tell us something."

"Bugger him."

"And look, there's someone else coming up the hill now. Over there, further down."

"I must have another word with my mother. Maybe there were triplets."

"Don't be silly. But that first one really *does* look like you."

"Never mind him," he says almost roughly, putting a hand on each of her shoulders, turning her round to face away from me. He stands on his high altar, looking his sacrificial victim in the eye. She returns his gaze, thinking he is about to kiss her. Through his eyes I see a closeup of her face and its moods – trust, expectation, slight concern at the unreadable expression in the face opposite. Through my eyes, I see them standing motionless above me, as if a statue of two lovers has been erected on the summit.

I push my body to the limit, continuing to wave, having no breath to shout. But her back is to me.

His hands are moving slowly inwards, along her shoulder blades, caressing the skin on her neck—

I stop looking for the easiest route and head straight for them, scrambling and slipping on all fours, up forty-five degrees of rock.

He is leaving her neck, cupping her chin, pulling her head gently towards him, lightly giving her the expected kiss. She is responding, her arms encircling his body, pulling herself against him.

I am now approaching the cone of rock on which they stand. But my climbing energy is spent, my reserves long since run out. She still has her back to me. For the moment I cannot go up any further, so I edge sideways along the hill, hoping to bring myself into her view.

Oblivious of me, they are continuing their embrace.

I am twenty feet below them. The slope between is just

climbable, but it might as well be a precipice. I draw in huge gulps of air. "Valerie— " My voice is a whisper, softer than the wind that threatens to blow my exhausted body off the face of the hill. But she is now facing in my direction, catches a glimpse of my figure appearing below, breaks partially free to look down at me, eyes widening as she sees a face identical to the one she has been kissing. "Valerie it's me. You know me. *He's* the imposter. Get away from him, he's a killer, he's— " But it is too late, the royal box is filled, the performance, too long postponed, can now begin. His hands are around her throat, he has begun to squeeze. I see them struggle above me, just out of reach, glowing golden in the noonday sun. I cannot bear it and shut my eyes, covering them with my hands. But there is no escape. Every element of his consciousness is projecting into me, at full power, at close range, and I cannot shut it off. The view from his eyes takes over and I see in closeup the succession of emotions that pass across her features – disbelief, betrayal, panic, fear of death, the lapse into unconciousness as her lovely face is transformed into a death mask. I feel his fingers on her neck as if they are my own, the pain of her ineffectual kicks against his shins. It seems as if my body has been taken over by an evil puppetmaster and I myself am committing the atrocity, a paralysed witness of my own actions. But, worst of all, I feel his spirit soar, springboarding from my despair, carrying off her soul, high above the peak on which he stands, away in triumph over the city; I hear his mocking laughter, in my mind and in my ears, as his hatred feeds upon my anguish.

She is dead. For a moment, he tries to cling on to that summit of ecstasy, to lock away that instant of joy and preserve it forever, but already he is falling to earth. He is merely a man, standing at the top of a mountain with a dead woman in his arms. Contemptuously, he flings the corpse down at me, and hurries off down the hill, in the opposite direction.

She rolls past me, coming to a stop a little further down the slope. I crawl after her and take her in my arms, frantically searching for some sign of life, finding none, weeping over her broken body.

I am still there when the sun clouds over and the first drops of rain fall upon us. I have not moved when the other man arrives, ignoring and resisting him as he gently tries to prize me loose from my charge.

TWENTY-FIVE

FROM THIS POINT ON my recollection becomes less clear. The other man – the climber Valerie had noticed earlier – helped me back down to the road, where we flagged down a passing car for help. My next memory is of being interrogated in the police station by Superintendant Montgomery and one of his assistants. My only remaining desire was to do what I should have done so many months before, help them clear up the strangler investigation once and for all. I told them everything that I have recounted in this narrative.

Considering the fantastic nature of so much of my story, I did not expect to convince them easily, and in view of my culpability on so many points, I was not expecting very much sympathy. Even so, their reaction took me by surprise. Instead of being treated as a valuable witness, they heard me out then locked me in a cell. Before long, I was brought out again and put in an identity parade. I was identified as the strangler of course, but I persisted with my story and Montgomery eventually yielded to my protestations sufficiently to visit my home. It was only on his return that the full horror of my predicament became clear.

"Did you see my wife?" I asked him.

"We've just been to see Mrs. Middleton," he said.

"Good. Where is she? Isn't she coming down to identify me?"

"No," said Montgomery. "We saw Mrs. Middleton *and* Mr.

Middleton. I admit that the resemblance between you and your brother is remarkable, and it was a neat trick to try and shift the blame on to him. Luckily for him, his wife is quite sure of his identity. He also has an alibi for four of the murders, and for the attempted murder in Portobello."

It took a while for his words to properly register. The killer was still impersonating me! Murdering my secretary was not enough; he had now moved in on my wife and family. I had to be forcibly restrained, as I tried to make Montgomery understand the danger that Jean and the children were in. His only reaction was to formally charge me with six murders.

And so they are keeping me here, an innocent man, while the killer walks free, taking over my life, living with my wife and family. So far he has made no move to harm them – he seems, in an almost touching way, to be deriving some comfort from this secure family home, of a kind he has never known before – but for how long can I be sure of their safety?

Our mental fusion has continued, and sometimes I find myself sitting at home, talking to Jean, living my own life through his senses. On other occasions he is here with me, sharing my prison cell, even helping me write this narrative. There are times when I feel that *I* am the one at home and *he* is in the cell. And who am "I" anyway? I am the responsible half of our joint personality, the one with human feelings, the one with a conscience. Once that was Edward Middleton, but now— It has all become very confusing. There are times when I wonder if they have locked up the right man after all—

Sometimes I think that we are both equally guilty, or equally innocent. We began life as equals, identical human beings with the same potential. How easily could our positions have been reversed, with he being sent to the loving home and I to the orphanage. What a small turn of fate could have made him the respectable city lawyer and me the strangler! And how can I disown his homicidal lusts when I have found them within me as well?

The only fact of which I am certain is that, as long as I live, I will see the faces of those dead girls, hear their death gasps, suffer the grief of their families. And he now feels the same. But the burden is not lessened by being shared, and I do not know how much longer I can bear the pain of it.

EDITOR'S POSTSCRIPT

THE DAY AFTER HE COMPLETED the above document, Cunningham was found hanging in his cell. While not entirely sure what to make of the narrative, the police thought it raised enough questions to merit another interview with the murderer's twin brother, Edward Middleton. They found that he had killed himself in the same manner at, so far as they could tell, virtually the same time as his brother.

Two more facts merit attention. Firstly, the reader may wonder, since it is established that the murderer did have a twin brother, whether the wrong man could really have been arrested. This possibility was thoroughly checked by the police, and there can be no doubt of the truth – the prisoner's clothing, the contents of his pockets, his dental records, all confirm it. It was definitely Henry Cunningham who went voluntarily to the police, who was charged with the murders and who wrote the above narrative in prison. And the man living with Mrs. Middleton was indeed her husband.

The last fact is the most curious of all. As confirmed by the narrative, Middleton had alibis for several of the murders, his whereabouts during the second one being vouched for by many members of the Edinburgh legal profession, including a judge. However, he had no alibis for the final two, even his wife being unable to account for his movements on those days. Moreover, David Thorne, the man who found Cunningham with the body of Valerie Mackinnon, is adamant that there were two other men on Arthur's Seat that day. He claims that he witnessed the murder, and that the killer remained in his clear view as he made off down the hill afterwards. He is certain that it could not have been the same man that he later found with the body and accompanied to the police station, the man subsequently identified as Cunningham. But Thorne was still some way off at the time of the murder and the police are convinced that he must have been mistaken. How his testimony would have been received in court must remain a matter of speculation.

The reader will have to decide for himself what the truth is. The police have taken the pragmatic attitude that the murderer is definitely dead and that the case should be regarded as closed.

FICTION

McGROTTY AND LUDMILLA
by Alasdair Gray.

" *... very funny, and keeps up a cracking pace throughout.*"
— Moira Burgess, THE SCOTSMAN
£5.00 (pbk) ISBN 1 872536 00 X

BLOODING MISTER NAYLOR
by Chris Boyce.

" *... rough-hewn, streetwise and sinister.*"
— Alan Taylor, THE LISTENER
£5.00 (pbk) ISBN 1 872536 04 2

GENERAL

LORD BYRON'S RELISH
The Regency Cookery Book
by Wilma Paterson.

" *... perhaps the best contribution to gourmet literature since
Gunter Grass eulogised the humble potato.*"
—Ian Bell, THE OBSERVER
£7.50 (pbk) ISBN 1 872536 02 6

A SENSE OF SOMETHING STRANGE
Paranormal Investigations
by Archie E. Roy.

" *... can only prompt wonderment and question in the reader
with an open mind.*"
— Susy Dale, THE OBSERVER
£7.50 (pbk) ISBN 1 872536 06 9

POETRY

FINDRINNY
by Donald Goodbrand Saunders

" ... a voice to be reckoned with, a mature, sensitive poet."
— Joy Hendry, THE LISTENER

£4.50 (pbk) ISBN 1 872536 08 5

TRAMONTANA
by Hugh McMillan

"poems of great insight, self-knowledge and feeling.
— Ian Crichton Smith

£4.50 (pbk) ISBN 1 872536 11 5

THE ABOVE ARE AVAILABLE FROM:
Bookspeed, 48a Hamilton Place, Edinburgh EH3 5AX
031-225 4950

OR DIRECT FROM:
Dog & Bone, 175 Queen Victoria Drive, Glasgow G14 9BP
041-959 1367